MAIDEN

D0950919

MAIDEN

CYNTHIA BUCHANAN

QUILL
WILLIAM MORROW
NEW YORK

Copyright © 1972 by Cynthia Buchanan

Grateful acknowledgment is made to Dwarf Music for permission to quote from
the lyrics of *Sad-Eyed Lady of the Lowlands* by Bob Dylan, copyright © 1966
by Dwarf Music; and to Atzal Music, Inc., for permission to quote from the lyrics
of *Take Her Out of Pity* by Bob Shane, Nick Reynolds, and John Stewart,
copyright © 1961 by Atzal Music, Inc.

All rights reserved. No part of this book may be reproduced or utilized in any form
or by any means, electronic or mechanical, including photocopying, recording, or
by any information storage or retrieval system, without permission in writing from
the Publisher. Inquiries should be addressed to Permissions Department, William
Morrow and Company, Inc., 1350 Avenue of the Americas, New York, N.Y. 10019.

It is the policy of William Morrow and Company, Inc., and its imprints and affili-
ates, recognizing the importance of preserving what has been written, to print the
books we publish on acid-free paper, and we exert our best efforts to that end.

Library of Congress Cataloging-in-Publication Data is available.

ISBN 0-688-16789-6

Printed in the United States of America

First Quill Edition 1999

1 2 3 4 5 6 7 8 9 10

www.williammorrow.com

To My Mother

With your sheets like metal and your belt like lace
And your deck of cards missing the jack and the ace
And your basement clothes and your hollow face
Who among them could think he could outguess you?
With your silhouette when the sunlight dims
Into your eyes where the moonlight swims
And your match-book songs and your gypsy hymns,
Who among them would try to impress you?

BOB DYLAN

1

She was a virgin and her virginity had burrowed in. So she was a little crazed, a little abstract . . . looked for symbols, answers, messages everywhere. And anxious, she knew such anxiety. It may be that all virgins feel this. Her virginity and her anxiety made her a daydreamer, a planner, a struggler, too gay, too earnest. Would life forget about her? Overlook her? Pass her by? Misdial? Anxiety became a life style.

She lived in an envelope. Sometimes she had trouble noticing things other people did. At other times she saw only too well. One thing she noticed was herself, in light of her own daydreams. These were not airy, sentimental hallucinations, but deep, mournful pageants in her bloodstream. She made a fetish of herself. Her personality grew more baroque, surprised her at every turn. Yet she continued to be her own friend. She consulted herself, admired her own opinions, asked advice of her own wisdom. She had a native integrity, a sense of self, which protected her. But she thought too often to play the *grande dame* on the strength of it. While people went on not noticing her. To the point of overkill. And she continued lusting for their approval, their esteem, their warmth.

At thirty, the idea of sex had such a grip on her that she

1

tried to avoid, totally, thinking about sex. It was a void in her reality and her curiosity minced around it—so high you cannot get over it, so low you cannot get under it. This void obsessed her but she denied her obsession and her curiosity. On the other hand, it seemed she was somehow always hunkering around the spoor of this torrid, nameless chimera. She followed it all in raw movies and magazines . . . in parks, once, and once on a beach she had spied on a couple. But it was still as remote, as irrelevant as Communism or cancer.

She admitted one thing to herself, however: she was looking for a man. She sure was looking for some man. Yet she always looked in private, so secretly that she nearly hid her desperate search from herself altogether.

She worked hard on her image. She was convinced it served her well. Her airs drew on the cinema, on the 1950's, on Loretta Young, on Ann Blyth, on the mannered billowing, too, from fiction—Blanche Dubois, Jean Brodie. She had no idea how false she was.

The extravagant daydreams possessed her, she went soaring off on them. Clothes possessed her. Her wardrobe came from a mail-order catalogue, Frederick's of Hollywood . . . tufts, spangles, synthetic animal skins. Clothes spoke to her; inanimate things often did. She might be walking through a department store. A dress—always one with a rhinestone geegaw or something that fluttered—would cry out, *Me! Me! Buy me!* She wore the clothes, thinking herself distinct and magic. Meanwhile, her affectations, her rouged grimaces . . . these were misread by people everywhere. (But when she got to Los Angeles, her peacock behavior and arch clothing helped her fade like a chameleon into the cityscape along Sunset Strip.)

2

Language haunted her. The advertised word . . . the "you" in advertising, the impossible "you" spoke to her. It was part of the summons, part of the superstition that seduced her daily. Human experience and earthly lessons glanced off her like a defracted ray. Yet inanimate objects held secrets. In an employment office a year ago, an ad, "California," had been part of the summons. There was superstition in everything.

It was all there, the truth. It was there in the hints about charm, from booklets. (One of the maxims: *Be Yourself!* Then she found she was often punished for this.) In the raw belief . . . the voodoo of her personality.

She moved perpetually in this gossamer sac of musing and advertising. She was waiting for the summons, the tap on the shoulder, the visitation, the different drums. When people spoke to her, she listened for all these, straining for the drums. The speaker might be part of the design watching her, approving, about to approve. . . .

A man, impossibly smitten, an individual so love-sick he can scarcely walk, stumbles toward her. His arms are outstretched. In his hands, an amphora; in this vase is love. He says: Fortune Dundy, where have you been all my life? He has come to salvage and endorse her. Everyone always knew she had it in her; what she called "a certain subterranean something." She had nothing upon which she based all this except autosuggestion.

The gleam of the summons was all around her. In the disclosures of daydreams. In the stares of strangers . . . all potential truthmongers. Hope lay heavily within her, corroding. Then it would give way and doubt came around. And again, hoping. Such a pinwheel of alternating hope and doubt kept her slightly beyond presence of mind. It made her happy and addled in the daytime hours. She was waiting. The intensity of this was awful. The weight of her atrophying sensuality grew. In the dark in her bed she tussled with faith and desperation. She remembered how she was then. And her maidenhood was seen floating like a kite high above a topography that seemed real, that seemed important to other people. She knew she was . . . gauche, denied it, contended with it. And lying there awake in bed, the pleasant muddle of daytime hours would then leave her.

Jobs! The past! Helter-skelter stints that left her panting like a rabbit. Dreaming and waiting for buses, watching, forgetting . . . Finesse in the world of business: this was one of her ideas. To be a crackerjack, glib sort of person. With sparkle. Sparkle was marketable. Employers knew this! But a person had to wait and watch and, most of all, improve. She studied the hidden secrets in the backs of magazines, panting over the promises. And always she sensed the love-struck man. He read over her shoulder. He neither breathed nor moved; he just skimmed the print.

As for this smitten man . . . she would not accept just any. Was this America? Does a person settle for second best? Just any would not do. For one thing: no Adam's apple, nobody with one of those.

Sometimes the stricken man grabbed her into a corner, into the gloamings of the potted palms. This is where you stop dancing, lady, he says. You have got that certain subterranean. I have got plans to listen to every word you say. Not because you have got a lot to say. But because I like the way you say it, dammit. And also I would like to tell you at this time that I will put my arms around you at random. And if there is a thunderstorm outside at night, we will work that

4

out too. Everything is going to be A-O.K. One more question: Tell me . . . where have you been all my life?

Her experience with men was limited. Their interest in her amounted to very little. Or so things had proved themselves. There lay the problem.

True enough, one or two scrubby boyfriends had reared their heads a long time ago. But she was not a woman, one of those who always have someone, some parasite or some goon who needs her. She was a woman who seemed as if she had somebody . . . he waited for her out back at the end of a working day. She appeared that way. But, actually, she had no one. And having no one at all made it harder and harder, as time went on, to have anyone at all.

She would not admit she was alone. She did not realize or articulate her solitariness. But the opaque fact of it fed upon her. For a long time she pretended men were unimportant. Then finally she admitted their consequence; this idea, too, was still obscure. Ultimately: men were the other half of existence. No . . . they were *all* of it. For without a man a person had no measure—how could she weigh or define herself? She might wander forever, wondering to what extent she filled out her outlines.

She struggled to ignore all this. But sometimes her awareness of men hung around her in a mist. In the presence of a certain kind of man, she reduced herself to her silhouette. She laughed and gasped and blurred—what an explosion! And in time the men—the scrubby boyfriends, too—retreated. They went to a calmer corner of the universe. That the men retreated she could not avoid knowing. But she did not see the reasons for it. And she made things worse. And knowing but not knowing undermined them still more.

What sort was she? She knew exactly who she was. It only remained to tell the world. "Bert"—Bert Parks of the Misses America, "Bert" the emcee—was a device of hers. He knew who she was. He lurked in her vapors. "Bert" stood for any emcee, any interrogator, any reporter, any judge or juryman, any person or thing whose sole interest was her. Whose sole purpose was to examine her, discover, present her, and venerate her. "Bert" meant the way things should be. "Bert" was the voice of her playful, high-strung narcissism.

She fought often but not openly with "Bert." He came into her brain at times of stress . . . but, evilly, he came to stir up a vision even in her idleness. "Bert" was one voice and all of them . . . a thousand messages, reminders, chimeras, critics, and promises. And he had lived in her brain such a long time now. He was company, bitter and loving. His presence was like a persona. "Bert" was her different drummer. He pummeled her spirit without rationale. He took forms . . . inhabited her, incubus, succubus . . . she was always being interviewed or questioned or complimented and then left to doubt the praise. Examined . . . sometimes it was a courtroom. Other times in a contest, a review, or on television or in a movie. Bert, all Berts, were only too aware of her exalted place, her focus in the public eye.

So she waited for courtly love. An awful, abstract, improbable lover! Someone on whom she might test her disdain.

The atrophying sex . . . the fantasies—it had all become almost perverse. She was like a drugged woman. And she went on carrying it . . . this calcifying fetus, the burden of her solid maidenhead.

2

TO ALL MY FRIENDS AND ACQUAINTANCES AND
THEIR KINDRED SORROWS AND EVERYONE ELSE
WHO HELPED MAKE ALL THIS POSSIBLE: Good
evening. Good evening to you all, she says.

He requests she speak into the microphone. The "mike."
He leans with her, says, "And who have we got with us
tonight! Say hello to a thirty-year-old bundle of sparkle—
Fortune Dundy! Tell the folks out there . . ."

ATTRACTIVE PERSON WITH SPARKLE: The first thing I did,
    Bert? I put a higher type pronunciation on my first
    name. You have got to keep an eye on the last "e" in
    my Christian name.

HE: Fortune?

ATTR. PRSN. W/SPRKLE.: No. Fortunée. Rhymes with have-
    your-say.

HE: Why . . . Fortunée . . . say, that is French!

ATTR. PRSN. W/SPRKLE.: Yes, Bert, I am afraid it is!

HE: Sing it on out now, Fortunée Dundy!

ATTR. PRSN. W/SPRKLE.: Being new to California myself
    . . . and by the way, Bert, they surely did "break the
    mold," like they say, when they made this Golden
    State! . . . in the coffee shop at Hollywood and

Vine, around in there. He was wearing a pair of bright and very tight pants. Bleached blond streaks run through his hair and he is a coiffure artist, he tells me, in the Eleganza Salon. Well, I will not "bluff" with you, yes, I did take to him. Then he walked, dancing kind of, over to the cigarette machine for a package of Virginia Slims. He was thin as a little tree snake. The way he walked to the cigarettes, by that time I was thinking: you are nobody's fool. Meaning me . . . I am nobody's, you have got to get up pretty early in the morning to . . . and then he walked on out of the coffee shop. Left me spinning on my stool. And him not fish, not fowl! Rude? Rude, you say? Mister, you do not know!

HE: Sorry to hear this. . . . Would you move a bit closer, just a millimeter, thank you, Fortunée. You know, you look "like a million dollars" in mauve! You . . . that color every day of the year!

ATTR. PRSN. IN MAUVE: I would just like to tell our crowd here tonight I am not a person that gets "down in the mouth" easily.

HE: No, sir!

ATTR. PRSN. IN MAUVE: Clear what I needed. Sunshine, suntan. I told myself, miss, what you need is one of those brown-as-a-berry suntans, one of those California berry-brown suntans. You might think I am just a . . . but I keep my eyes open, you can bank your money on these two baby blues being open. To the Pacific . . . and I crossed the highway, almost did *not* cross, with it burning into my feet and the cars, they do not care if you are on your way to the beach or if you have got to wait with your feet on fire and the first sand of the beach is no different, but mostly those cars did not slow down or give an inch. Broken glass, parked cars, a snack stand—and there it is! As far as a person's eye can see: bodies stretched and flat and browner than syrup. Bodies everywhere . . . collapsed there like string puppets, oiling themselves and also their neighbors' backs. And then, of course, you have got your typical teen-age girls that are like women but you know they are younger. Just a word here, Bert, about lifeguarding in California: they sit up there perching, these men, these lifeguards, wearing their sunglasses in a way that *does* make them look like they could save your life better. The only way you could ever get these lifeguards to look down from their tower is to drown. That is an old, old joke we women know. Then I walked on through these shining puppet bodies in the sun. I excused myself. You might think I do not know . . . "Beg pardon," I kept saying. I was wearing this swimsuit you see here, mauve. No, true, it is not like their suits. Mine has got its own personality and individuality. See this little skirtlet here around the bottom? This skirtlet gives it . . . "sass" and individuality. I could not take a solitary step, no, I was squishing suntan oil out of somebody's tube . . . have you ever been to Santa Monica Beach on a summer day? . . . or spraying sand in somebody's chiliburger. Then . . . found . . . this young middle-aged person on his back. Pestering a little Zenith radio, its dial. Next to . . . staked out my towel. He said exactly nothing

to me at that time. I sat down on my towel . . . I
also said nothing . . . could almost hear the sun, it
was that hot. He . . . next door rummaging in his
beach bag, pestering the Zenith. I sat up. I looked out
at the water . . . like this. Maybe he would wonder,
beg pardon, but who is that mystery woman fixing
her bead so deep. He said exactly nothing. I ran my
fingers through my hair, like this . . . aaaaaah, feels
good! This wind! This beach, this sun! But he, at that
time, said zero. Then I looked . . . at him. He had
this wristwatch tattooed on his wrist. A joke! Do you
believe me? It is true! So for a joke—and for "an
opener," like they say—I lean over and I say in a voice
like this: Beg pardon, could please happen to tell a
person the time? Him? He lifted up his sunglasses for
a minute. I point to the tattoo. He curls up his lip . . .
turns up the radio music . . . it was a song I could
sing for you . . . is that it? The tune? La la ba ba ba
bum bum . . . that it? Thank you! No, Bert, no, I do
not do it professionally . . . just in the shower . . .
my own pleasure . . . no, I would not want to go
pro, thank you for offering . . . and he laid his head
back down! Well, Bert, I tried to laugh. But that
laugh gurgled and died in my throat. That ever
happen to you? Sun went behind a cloud of something . . . folded up his towel and radio, the individual with the joke on his wrist that he did not want
the world to laugh about. He goes to leave. He steps
over . . . and listen to this . . . my legs. Down he
leans, he leans down, his Our Mary medals dangling
down. He says to me: "Say, now, proxy-locks, you

10

would not want a lay, would you?" I sit up. I smile. My first inclination—do not laugh at this—to take him to mean . . . Hawaiian lei. But you have got to get up pretty early . . . morning to fool a person such as myself. He left. I was "dying a thousand deaths," like they say. Then, at our end of the beach, only me and . . . this one couple are left. On the beach. Sun's gone. Three people, me and them. They were standing up. The wind was blowing out her hair. It was so long . . . he could wrap his hands in it. And he did. Then he wrapped it . . . just so . . . like this . . . around her neck. Then he wrapped her up in the blanket. And then he wrapped his arms around her. Mister, something was trying to crack. Something in me, something small . . . like a bird's egg. And that voice, goddamn it, beg pardon the French, to the fires of . . . took me out to California in the first place, it started talking again. It talked straight this time. It said, "Fortune Dundy, life is passing you by, Fortune. It is passing you by, sister, faster than a fifty-dollar mare at a Fourth of July match race!"

(And, no, I do not feel sorry for my path in life, so you can put that in your pipe.)

❋

She went upstairs to her room and read "I Said 'No' a Minute Too Late" from *Modern Love Story* and then all of the *Los Angeles Times*. She tried new makeup tricks and danced with the door of the closet. While she danced, her

cheek hugging the wood, she thought of the distant sun trying to come through the city nimbus. The sun landed on
houses in bonbon colors, in backyards on broken tricycles
and garden tools rusting like junk art in rubber play pools
. . . patios . . . pubescent saplings; and always armies of
children, little people and their spaniels who choked sub-
urbia . . . plundering the saplings, carrying off their arma-
ture of nylon cord and doweling, stripping their branches for
play whips, and the bus had passed along a eucalyptus can-
yon silver and green . . . and sometimes the leaves shifted
like a school of fish. Her thoughts were cold in her cheeks.
Her song tonight was "Deep Purple." She embarrassed herself singing. But she sang on anyway, sheepish, glazed, per-
forming for herself.

After arrival at the terminal, she had locked herself in a
stall in the ladies' room. She had changed from something
into something . . . a new pair of mauve pants maybe. She
forgot to remove the dangling price tag. She was listening
to the first sounds of California: piped-in announcements of
buses departing. San Diego, Riverside, Phoenix.

At the Hotel Paris—ƧIЯAꟼ ꞱƎTOH on the glass door—she
danced and read.

Learn Good English! How to Be Popular! Old favorites:
Magic No-Strap Hidden-Suspension Plastic Cups to Clamp
Underneath Breasts, Cards with Eyebrow-Shaped Cutouts
to Trace-on Arches, Wallet-Size Photos, Chihuahuas That Fit
into a Teacup . . . she thought, what about an ad like this:
Backs of Magazines!

How to Be Popular: she had sent for the booklet, studied
it, a long time ago. She practiced the principles of eye-play
and those of handshaking . . . difficult as it was to shake

one's own hand, it could be done. And topical conversation . . . neatness in dress . . . it all seemed like a blueprint for somebody else's existence. But, anyway, let us keep dancing . . . *"Blue Moon . . . you knew just what I was there for. . . ."*

She went prowling into some nearby bars. In the darkness she sidled up to large-pored men and slipped away again, unannounced. She walked back to the hotel with the name backward from inside . . . bar smells in her head and handkerchief.

. . . makes a person embarrassed. Like the parties she goes to. She stands there alongside the militia of nuts and mints and napkins . . . guests too coy, too dull, people who are shells. Are there people who are shells? She stands at the party. And unstrung, truehearted, she mans an alarm bell . . . by sounding the ice in her glass. Nobody at the party seems to know what she is talking about. And they certainly pay no attention to the ice-cube alarm, none at all. Then what exactly did she come for? Young lady, why did you come to this foolish party? She came to find a man. But he is never there. And so all the planning what to wear and the primping make her a fool. Is there anything worse? A jackass who came to a party to debase herself in the company of shells?

Yet she keeps on coming to the party. This is what troubles her.

❋

Are You Lonely? STOP!!!

You Never Will Be Again!

DATAMATE first and foremost Blah Blah in California We Use the IBM 360 for Our Guaran-

13

teed Blah Blah Blah People Are for Loving!
Singles Widowed Divorced Blah Blah Blah!

She sent away.

Take a Few Minutes to Read This Message!

Every Word Is Important to YOU!

1. This is NOT a game.

2. If compatible friendship and/or a more meaningful relationship is not your goal, please do not use this questionnaire, as it is designed for all sincere and mature people seeking same.

3. If you are orthodox, devout, or sincere in your religion, please circle your answer of "2" to Question #8 on the Personality Answer Sheet.

4. Answer "7" to Question #8 greatly broadens the volume of names from which to select your matches.

5. Please DO NOT use anything but numbers in answering the questions—with the exceptions of Questions #5, 6, 12, and 72. (We will code these here.)

6. For servicemen *only:* Our IBM cards are limited to 18 characters (including spaces) on the ADDRESS LINE.

7. *Please* notify us immediately when you become involved, engaged, or otherwise committed to what appears to be more than a short-term relationship.

8. Many who have had experiences with Acquaintance-Dating and/or Matrimonial Computing wonder how we can do so much for only forty dollars. The answers are on Page Nine.

✦

14

To Who It Might Concern at DATAMATE: Your question about Additional Comments in this space is an interesting space to leave because I did want to say at this time about your question #72 that is not really your business #72 Yes or No Previous Sexual Exp. that do not think because of my answer I have got the Bible in mind I have not the Bible is too bossy is my opinion I am not saying #72 is a sin or the Fires of Hell no it is just that my opinion of my thinking I remember Wilma Sloan in my city every place has got a girl like that and even though on the "stage and screen" this year a person can see anywhere anytime people on top of the other person that naked and squirming does not mean "the eye of a gnat" as for naked it these days is "a dime a dozen" just walk down to Spring Street or Main Street at the bookstores and racks and do not think that just because I said that in #72 that I do not know "what end is up" Hop McElroy is one person you would be interested about eleven years ago and why is it men kiss and then get busy with you There and There when you only want to think about the kiss is what makes a person feel not lonely in answer to your ad Are You? You are going to say to me men do not bother with those "frills of life" they get to business but the person you DataMate has got in mind for me has got to think frills first business second if you get what I mean I know what I have got in mind and he will know too when he sees me too you will do well to keep that in mind when you are computing

F. Dundy

✿

Two blocks away they found coffee and pie. That was when Murray Caruthers said: "So . . . you're La Dundy."

"Yes. I surely am. Walking, talking in the flesh and new around here. How about yourself, Murray?"

"Yeah."

Murray Caruthers wore a small gardenia in his buttonhole. That opened her eyes right away. And even though she went on talking, ". . . yes, they surely did 'break the mold' . . ." she noticed the gardenia, in ecstasy. Blue Moon, you knew! Who wore a gardenia these days? Whoever it was, he took her to a movie, Faye Dunaway and Marcello Mastroianni, where Marcello drove a race car and Faye climbed the cyclone fencing to tell him she was interested. But Murray shifted and squeaked so much in his seat . . . usher *shush*ed him. Murray said to her: "I'll wait for you at the popcorn machine . . . *where there ain't so many Gestapo ushers!*" The last part in a loud voice.

Then the coffee and pie. And then: "So . . . you're . . . La Dundy."

"Yes, I certainly am. Walking, talking in the flesh and new around here. How about yourself, Murray?"

"Yeah."

"Beg pardon?" she said.

"I don't know why when a man asks for blueberry pie they bring you this crap. Look at that, will you? It looks like something some dog threw up."

"Let me see."

"I didn't think I was asking for the world on a silver platter when I asked if they had any homemade blueberry pie, did you?"

"No."

"Was it too much to ask?" he said.

"Would you be interested in a trade? I only bit the end off mine. It is very tasty. It is peach. Peach pie. Look."

"I don't want your pie. Why would I take your pie away from you?"

"Oh, do you think I mind? Please. Try it! I like blueberry. I will eat yours."

"You'd eat something some dog threw up?"

"I really do not mind."

"Miss! Miss! Waitress! Sssssst!"

"Please!" Fortune said. "It is all right by me! Here . . . look! Peach! Try it!"

Murray gave her a long, ripe look then, moving his eyes over her face. He imbedded them finally in her eyes. "You know how to cook?" he said.

"Certain sorts of things."

"Miss! Miss! You, miss! *Sssssssst!*"

In bed she winnowed through the events of The Murray Caruthers Affair. Superstition crackled in her brain. She had jinxed him. He never called again. Her two lies . . . How many, Miss Dundy? Two, Bert. How many, Miss? Two, I said! Hold the telephone, Miss Dundy: to begin with, there was the information about . . . the "modeling" assignment, if we are not mistaking.

Then let us not begin.

Step a snatch closer, Miss Dundy, and share with us how you first began to "weave your wicked web."

She had lopped off two inches on her own height. *Height?* said the DataMate application. And here at last was deception's own seed coming back at her. A lie had a life of its own. Free as a goblin, it would flit at night near the bed. Hold the telephone, not one lie, but two. Which of them had Murray seen shadowed beneath the ledges of her eyelashes? So you were false two times, then, Miss Dundy? . . . each Regina Lashes "Real Hair" sitting on your eyelids like furry caterpillars!

And beg pardon, Miss Dundy. We were going over this file of yours, DataMate's little monthly checkup to see facts are facts. Your college? You . . . what? You have got the diploma somewhere but cannot . . . beg pardon? Sixty seconds to go . . . oh-oh! There it goes! And we *are* sorry!

*

The time came to get her money's worth. She had been remembering Tibshraeny Office Supplies painted on the side of Murray's car. But instead she finally telephoned Data-Mate.

A widowed engineer came. Jack Gandemutt from Jet Propulsions Laboratories. But he wore nothing in his buttonhole. Jack took her to an apartment in Alhambra, where middle-aged people were fussing over marijuana cigarettes and talking about going to watch the submarine races on Signal Hill. They were showing off for one another, dancing to old Harry Belafonte records: Day-oh! Day-ayaaaaaaaaa-oh! Jack had prinked at his reflection in the stainless-steel trim on the elevator. He held her hand when he rang the doorbell.

During the evening, Jack followed a woman named Inez. He kept popping back to Fortune on the couch, with a whispered and highly intimate burr of a question: "Having a good time, cookie?"

18

Inez stationed herself behind the Clydesdale buttocks, two immense, apple-shaped things. Fortune had become rather transfixed by those oaken thighs and that immutable, draft-horse rear end of Inez's. And Jack was always there in the vicinity of Inez's fumes. No surprise then this: In a parking spot at the Paris, Jack turned off the key in the ignition. He doubled Fortune's fist into his hand. "You're a woman, aren't you? Tell me: what do you women want?"

"Your question is you want me to tell you my opinion on what us women want?"

"Want! Want! One day you say one thing. And the next day . . . what in God's name do you want of a man!" Jack put his head down on the steering wheel. He strained against the diagonal safety belt on his chest.

She was wearing a friendship ring that night. Jack had squeezed her hand so hard it pinched the ring and bent it up against her other finger.

He cried in big wet rubber sounds . . . hunching his shoulders, squeezing her ring hand harder, banging it lightly on his knee. "She's so . . . high-minded! What business does she have acting that way? I want to see her settle down into the kind of life she deserves! Woman of her caliber deserves marriage! Oh, God!" Then he had leaped out of the car and bustled Fortune to the Paris door. He mashed her hand a final time and bounded off into the neon night, his pocket change and car keys the only sound she remembered. Daaaa-aaaa-oh! Da-dee-da-day-ay . . . oh.

She watched the California women . . . for a clue. Teenagers born of sea-foam and shower stalls, barefoot, in a hurry, their eyes bright with youth or drugs . . . nubilia on its way to where? Where are you going? Where are those women going? Back to the sea? Screen tests? Cheerleading practice? Devil worship? "College-'n-Career"-age girls passed in bright cotton, long steps. In suede fringe, in fringed hair, in huge helmets of electrified hair, dirty girls, beautiful girls passed. Fortune studied The Divorced Look . . . its Plexiglass glamour and ivory hair . . . it adjusted huge pale sunglasses behind windows of air-conditioned Thunderbirds . . . and there were cocktail waitresses who followed their Beverly-hillock breasts, shopping at noon in charm bracelets.

A brochure arrived in the mail. It was from Dionysus West, Incorporated, founders of DataMate. It was a "singles" club for people over twenty-five. ". . . *Life begins where they leave off! The* Real *Generation Gets It Together! So . . ."*

Now That You've Tried DataMate
(one of our ever-growing subsidiaries)

WHY NOT . . . ?
GO DIONYSUS WEST, YOUNG SWINGLE! *

* You there between the ages of twenty-five and forty!
* You there looking for rollicking, frolicking friendship,
dateship, mateship!
!Punch-uate the Story of Your Life!
Year-round Bacchus Bashes! The Fun
Scene! The Sun Scene! Parties!

Dances! Dinners! Picnics!
Celebrations! Clambakes!
and Wienie Roasts!

Sea Weekends! Ski Weekends!
Skoal Brothers! Skoal Sisters!

JOIN THE BIGGEST AND BRIGHTEST SINGLES
SET IN THE WEST AND FOLLOW THE SUN
TO WHERE SWINGER MEETS SWINGER
IN THE EYE OF THE

! A C T I O N !

——Membership includes all the above PLUS:——

1. —Free subscription to our monthly, *The Grapevine.*
2. —Free copy of *The Dionysus Dateline,* the quarterly
   catalogue of members' names, addresses, phone
   numbers, occupations, hobbies, pix.
3. —Discounts at the DW Boutique (DW sweatshirts,
   bumper stickers, tie clasps, blazers, cocktail napkins . . . and a host of other Dionysus West
   paraphernalia!).
4. —An opportunity to participate in the Dionysus West,
   Inc., profit-sharing plan.
5. —An opportunity to live in dynamic

VILLA DIONYSUS
"Where the Scene Gets Together"

FOR COMPLETE DIONYZATION, ALL YOU NEED
DO IS FILL IN THE FOLLOWING:

❀

There were photographs of sunning, skiing, joshing people. Hey! Hi! Ho! They hailed the camera . . . a wave, a
lifted glass, V-fingers . . . Hey!

21

3

Inside the recreation hall notices were tacked on a "Bacchus Bulletin Board" . . . "Baccy sez: For sale Amad Jamal albums. Attn: Please all Dionysids to buy raffle tickets win Mustang. Attn: Please while in pool not to leave laundry in washers after they have finished cycle. LOST Doberman Pinscher answers to name of Tulip. NEED TO RENT SCUBA equipment. Fourth of July Bacchus Bash!!! BIG PRIZES! Best Costume Symbolizing America, Bitter Ones, Bland Ones. Gayle Richey, where are you? I'm sorry. 1948 Morgan in ace cond., spoke wheels, will sacrif. To Who It Might Concern: Hello I am a new gal in town also a new DW member looking for a roommate at Villa Dionysus I am attractive and pleasant and I would like to move in quick. F. Dundy."

A young woman named Beverly Besqueth called. They met at Newberry's lunch counter on a lunch break. Blah blah blah. Beverly was a person who wanted to help herself; she seemed to be a young woman with plans, action, ideas for self-improvement. She met with a "touch session" in East L.A. on Fridays. She talked as if she did not know what she was talking about, however. I said to her, "What do you mean?" and she said, "Oh, you know what I mean." Beverly had been a freshman Homecoming Princess at Orange Blah Blah Junior College . . . 1959 . . . had there really been a year 1959? It seemed more the title of a book . . . a song . . . a movie. 1959.

Beverly Besqueth was sage, round, looked like someone . . . who? Once she had been an airline hostess. The company went defunct . . . it was a small West Coast airline, losing money, going down, its planes were ghosts now. This was her twelfth year as a divorcée. She had been married at eighteen. "What a bastard. Would you believe I came out of that still punching? Christ-o. And I will tell you. I popped right into junior college though . . . then out six months later. I was a zombie . . . trying to forget him. But now I'm new, clean!" Beverly had met a new man. "And what a honey! Christ-o, wait'll you meet *him*. Now *he* knows how to take care of a little girl! I said to Miss Grumpet, 'We're well, Miss G.'" Beverly Besqueth had female problems . . . a uterus that the boyfriend had named Miss Grumpet . . . monthly blinding pain, fever, vomiting.

Beverly blinked when she did not understand. She had a nickname . . . from college or childhood . . . "Biscuit." She had said, "Biscuit'll do." She had met her new boyfriend at a dance on the Villa Dionysus tennis court. "He's in the ad business." It was a small firm, plucky, coming, her boyfriend was rescuing an account called Pudding Tain. Milo's idea was a tiny logo-nebbish, Li'l P.T. "He's very into this. Li'l P.T. could be a comic strip on each box of the mix! It would work into a whole TV series . . . a 'misadventures' sort of bit. He's still trying to push it through at the clients'. But those dudes don't know their ass from a hole in the ground. I mean, what're you going to do, you know?" She studied her Coca-

Cola glass. "He says the reason I have Miss Grumpet and her little gymnastics is my heart's too soft. I kept all my upsets inside, he says, and then Miss Grumpet has to pay the piper, you know?" (Fortune is already half in love with Milo Campbell.) "I have been very hung up over . . . Vivian. My last roommate. Her morals. How are yours, by the way? Vivian played hell on Miss G. Vivian—I mean, you know, my house is not a whorehouse! Christ-o, she can take her heads and her hang-ups and her hung-up boyfriends with her! I told her. I said, I'm not sharing rent on your sloppy . . . let me assure you . . . morals." Biscuit had told Vivian that she, Beverly, was not brought up under Vivian's standards and blah blah blah . . .

The music, the tense, female droning seeping blah blah blah from Biscuit's mouth . . . Fortune nearly missed the story for watching her mouth squirm and flex its story . . . a fascinating mouth, there was utter femaleness in it all. But she did not miss the story, no. It warmed her. It grounded her, welcomed her . . . and the man, this Campbell! Knew about a uterus! She loved Biscuit for being the sort of woman Milo would love; she loved Milo for loving Biscuit. Blah blah blah . . . how nice!

"I mean, she can take her crud and get out, I said. She did. Went to Vegas with her spaced-out drummer. Know what she did when she was dragging her suitcases out the door? She flipped this sign at me: ****. Yeah. That's what sort of a . . . would you believe after that one left it took days to get Miss Grumpet quieted. Emotion or cancer. One or the other."

"Oh my!"

24

"You're very into belts, aren't you? That's an interesting belt you have on there. Leopard, isn't it?"

"Well, not real leopard," Fortune said. "But it surely looks real, I would say. And versatile! Look. On this underside, this plain color. So I just flip it over . . . flip! . . . like this . . . and with your reversible buckle, then you have got yourself a whole new belt idea according to the outfit and color you are going to choose. I think it has got quite a lot of 'special touch' to it."

"Yes, indeed. Uhm, you don't have any steady boyfriend, do you?" Biscuit's mouth . . . the lips came to rest . . . lay like two nude bodies, languid, awaiting. . . .

Fortune said, "I was going with this one person, Murray Caruthers, a 'top banana' at one of the major firms on the West Coast, Tibshraeny, but you know, I got tired of him. His morals. I did not care too highly for his standards, you see. He was an executive. But do not be fooled."

"Vivian was not my kind of people," Biscuit said.

"I am inclined also to the 'no' side of that description of her you have just described to me about Vivian."

"Well," Biscuit bit down on a mouthful of ice . . . her tongue explored the fragments, "I think there's a slight . . ." Now she was spitting ice back into her glass, " . . . chance you might be my kind of people. And I'm going to tell Milo so. And maybe, just maybe, we three could be right happy in B-12. You and me and Miss G."

"Happy as punch!"

"Do you ever wear it turned over on the other side?"

"Not really. I always tell myself I am going to. But then in the end I generally end up with it turned leopard outwards."

"Well, it's very interesting. I'll bet it looks interesting with the plain color turned outside, too."

"Oh, it does. I just have not got around to it yet."

*

"All packed?" he said. "Christ-o, let's see if we can get this medicine show on the road! I've only been here since seven o'clock, you know!"

Biscuit's boyfriend was angry with Fortune. He had had to wait for her at her motel. Now his ill humor, dank, filled the car, filled her and made her cautious. He had come to pick her up at the Mountain Inn to move her to Villa Dionysus. (Biscuit: "Hey, I'll send the man in my life around." And Fortune had said: "Oh, say, you have not got to do that!" But: "Christ-o, no! You don't have to do anything but die. But I'm known around the Villa as Bleeding Heart herself. So pack up. . . .")

When Milo Campbell had knocked at the door of cabin Tetons there had been no answer.

"I was at the beach," Fortune told him now. She had been at the beach until dark, looking for the anklet lost in the sand. Marty, a sailor from the midway on the pier, he had won it for her the night before. Two silver hearts joined on a little chain. It was nighttime then too and once the anklet was lost on the beach . . . the jealous tide! . . . who could say where that anklet lay? Marty the Sailor was gone already, overseas on a ship. He would be hurt to think she had lost the silver anklet. The next day she had gone back to the beach to look for it. But by the time Mrs. Shortt's son, McGinnis, got her there, it was late afternoon . . . and then evening. The ugly tide, insidious and subtle as old age advancing, had come and gone. But would Marty the Sailor understand the tide's behavior? And she had no address, no long naval number, to write him and make him understand. "I was at the beach," she said again.

"Yes, dolly, I know," Biscuit's boyfriend said. His ear was cocked to the engine of the Morgan. And his eyes watched . . . were they watching? . . . his muttonchop whiskers in the rearview mirror. From time to time his eyes flicked to his hands on the steering wheel . . . the butterscotch driving gloves. He had knocked too at the cabin named Olympus and the cabin named Catskills. There had been a voice at the last. "Then this babe opens the door. I left the Morg running, thinking you must be around there someplace. The woman says, 'My boy McGinnis here just got out of the Army. He's hitting for Arizona with me to the Apache Junction mineral baths, he driv Fortune down to the beach.' And I say, 'Which beach?' See what I mean? Then she says to somebody coughing, your friend says, 'Which beach?' 'Shit,' the cougher says, 'Santa Monica, and me here trying to listen to the races and you whining drive her here, drive her there, find her a sugar titty, why don't I?' I mean, don't even ask me about it."

"That was my friend Mrs. Shortt's son, McGinnis," said Fortune.

"Very bright cat, McGinnis. Christ-o, it's a wonder I'm not there still knocking at doors right now."

Then abruptly he began talking about something else . . . the Fourth of July party coming up. He seemed, though, to be addressing . . . himself? There had been a . . . fight? Biscuit had wanted to go dressed as George and Martha Washington. Milo wanted to go as something else, something violent, something protesty . . . Fortune could not be sure

27

of the man's monologue. What was more Americana than the Washingtons?—this, at least, Biscuit had said for certain. A fight and then finally they had agreed: yet, something more original than the Washingtons. They would go as the couple on the calendar, a painting of *American Gothic*. Farmer and wife—how . . . *America!* They had laughed and laughed. But before the laughter, Biscuit had fallen onto the couch and jammed her face into a pillow. "She's the cutest little bitch when she's mad. . . ." Milo reporting on his woman . . . Fortune was thoroughly unnerved by his slickness now . . . his Morgan car . . . his show biz mannerisms. Why was he . . . speaking to air? To him she was air.

"Brainstorm it!" he hollered now. "You put all your ideas in the pot. Everyone in the group contributes. If one member of the group says about any particular idea, 'No, that won't work,' or, 'No, that sucks,' then the group has to shout 'Killer Phrase!' The idea is to pool and then select the best." Biscuit had said, apparently, "I say we should go as the Washingtons, George and Martha, that's my idea." Campbell's idea had been The Grim Reaper and Statue of Liberty, balled and chained together. Biscuit to that had shouted Killer Phrase.

Fortune groped for the knees of her pants. She rested her hands there, staring at the veins, smoothing her knees, speaking. The Morgan slalomed in and out of three cars. "The idea is for everyone to throw in a costume idea?"

"To 'brainstorm,'" he said.

"The idea I put in is: why do you two not go as a painting of the Washingtons?"

The man never replied. She fell to searching her purse for the cigarettes. They were pastel, "Vogues." "Try a Vogue?" she said.

Still . . . he might have friends, Bert. Vil-la Di-o-ny-susssss. This person Milo Campbell might very well have friends . . . men with teeth square and white as houses, men of incredible sensitivity. Double Date! Four Swingles in a Convertible! Hats? Scarves? *Us?* You gotta be kidding! Naked heads in the wind! That is our motto. Monsoon? End of the world? We will give it hell and then some! Roll out the barrel! Hey . . . you . . . you, the slender one . . . how about a song, you backseat singer back there! Blow a little our way . . . Swing 'n Sway with Fortunée! Blue Moon, you saw me standing.

He slowed at a stoplight. Vloogle-vloogle. This was the sound of the engine, it vloogled and shimmied. Campbell listened to it. She cleared her throat and rearranged her legs . . . heady little car! "This baby," she tapped the dashboard, "has got a lot of 'torque.'" What he would say to her word —who knew? "Try a Vogue?" she said again.

"No, thank you, no."

"I like the lavender ones best." The wind blew out her match. It was the last. With care, deference, she replaced the cigarette in its flat box. She gazed out the window at idling cars . . . drivers scratching, waiting, smoking, smoothing their necks, examining boils, earlobes, hairlines. "La la la la lala," she said softly. An old man near the Mountain Inn had been whistling that . . . walking his dog, whistling "Greensleeves" to himself while the dog wee-weed on a rosebush.

The man, Milo Campbell, with the whiskers and gloves and virile bad humor . . . had he even noticed she was lighting her own cigarette? The slow, curt walk, the abstract speech . . . this man was unlocking now the door of B-12 with the key he seemed to own.

Somehow . . . later, a cloud of sex hung dizzily in the room.

Biscuit had flown in from somewhere . . . running on little rabbit feet, pirouetting, hurtling. She collapsed on Campbell's lap. She clutched a box. Inside were costumes . . . Farmer John and a wife. "Howdy doody!" This was what she had said. She had danced around the man like his own smell. "Howdy doody howdy howdy doody doody!" She kissed the top of his head. "Is Boy still mad at Girl?" she said.

Fortune was somewhere in the room. She was standing in the vicinity of her suitcases and belongings.

Campbell grabbed up Biscuit's hands as if to eat them. Was he really going to do it? His teeth are poised . . . his eyes roll upward in mock . . . or real? . . . "No?" Biscuit says. "No, Boy isn't mad at Girl? Because would you believe Girl broughtum surprise, broughtum costumes! Oh-oh . . . look at Girl! Been to interior decowating class and gotum powder sugar donuts all over herself!" She had brushed furiously at the front of her sweatshirt.

Campbell cried, "Hey, go easy on those!" He removed her hands and himself brushed at her breasts. "Boy will do that. You keep forgetting you're only made of sugar and spice."

Fortune was holding her box purse. She stared down at it and began to bang it by the handle; it chinked rhythmically, in chaos against her thighs. Biscuit and her boyfriend were on the floor now, tickling each other. Through the transparent plastic the powder-coated bowels of the purse winked . . . the hairbrush, the shredded Kleenex, the eyelash curler,

30

coins, and the round, gutted box of Angel Face powder. Biscuit and the man squeal . . . they gasp and rise. A lovers' moment. Fortune bangs the purse again and again. Now the other two are in the bedroom; they are trying on costumes.

By this time Fortune stood out on the balcony, still banging the plastic purse against her thighs. Biscuit cried out from the bedroom: "Roomie, do you . . ." her laugh sounded like a man drowning, ". . . know what he . . . what he hrarrgh hrarrgh hrarrrrrgh! . . . said, Roomie? He says we can go to the party as Adam and Eve! But that's not Americ —hragh hraargh hrarrrrgh!"

To answer your question, Bert: The man is brushing sugar off her.

It is the man's voice now, drowning: "Or topless and bottomless American waitress and waiter . . . errrgh! errrgh!"

"DADDY, *PLEASE!* Behave!" Biscuit squealed. "Roomie out there is going to think you're naughty." In a louder voice still, "Don't mind him, Room-o, I do have to keep a tight rein on this one, Christ-o. He likes to be off-color about once every six months. Hey, how do you like the old homestead?"

"Beg pardon?"

Biscuit appeared, calm, clothed. "I emptied out some drawers and half a closet for you."

"Beg pardon? Thank you." She remained on the balcony, banging her purse. Miss Dundy? Bert says. Miss Dundy . . . you all right?

"Daddy" whispered Biscuit.

"What, poopsie?"

"Miss Grumpet wants . . . Pudding Tain."

They were gone. The apartment was quiet except for a

stereo throbbing through a wall . . . next door. Judy Collins . . . Joanie . . . someone moaning about silver daggers or logging men.

✿

Fortune sat in the living room amid her packing. Two moons of perspiration dried at her armpits. She finished and waited and was lonely and began to worry about a costume for the Fourth of July party. It was late. How dark night was, how very dark! She left the apartment and went outside, across the vast courtyard. The apartment complex was vast, a quadrangle . . . lighted windows, doorways of light. Figures ducked in and out of them in the summer night, stood in silhouette, were part of the mystique confirmed. The swimming pool—a lighted lake, she had seen it, too, from the balcony—shimmered, silent and aqua, antiseptic. And the music everywhere . . . like Muzak, but something different from every doorway . . . *lay across your big brass bed. . . . your wig-hat, mama, 'cause we're goin'. . . . My lover was a logger! None like him today, if you'd pour whiskey on it . . . bale of hay! . . . Stay, lady, stay. . . .* Doors opened and closed.

He came out of some offices . . . there were brass plaques on the doors. There were some shops as well; Villa Dionysus was built flush up against some small businesses, an arcade.

So at Campbell's apartment, A Wing . . . A-36 . . . Fortune faked something. She dropped to the WELCOME mat . . . her purse contents strewn on the mat. How adroit! She pretended to gather up the spilled contents. The man, now approaching, was still several yards away. She gathered up Kleenex . . . lipstick. Here, miss, do let me give you a hand

32

with that. Say . . . am I mistaking or . . . are you new around here?

The man walked on by her. He said nothing. Behind Milo Campbell's door, she heard a refrigerator door slam.

Who was the man passing in the night? Was there a message in the way the yellow light along the railing shone on his thin, misty hair? Maybe she should have spoken first . . .

Beg pardon, Miss Dundy!

I said: Maybe I should . . .

Beg pardon . . . ? Do not tell us you have forgotten so soon! Rule Number Nix: Let the Man Begin the Tlkg!

Are you saying I was . . . forward, Bert?

Miss Dundy, I am saying nothing. It is your throat you are cutting. Right, Your Honor?

Refrigerator sounds—bottles, drawers, ice trays—came through the door now. And a conversation:

"Would you believe your toes look like little pink peas."

"Would you believe your chest looks like hair. It looks hairy nice."

"You're beautiful. Would you believe . . . tweak tweak!"

"Ouch! Ouch! So are you. Um-um-um-um, I mean, you're *handsome!*"

"Say uncle . . . hey . . . wow, Christ-o . . . say uncle . . . you're really into this sado-maso stuff, aren't you?"

"Daddy . . . do you really truly like the Gothic pants?"

"Outa sight. We'll walk off with first prize."

"If Bob and Katy don't do it first. They're going as war dead. And you know . . ."

"Uncle?"

"But we're going every bit as—*uncle! yeeps, uncle!*—as their old war dead, huh, Daddy?"

"You betchum."

"And almost as good as George and Martha . . . aaaaa-aarh! Christ-o!"

"Biscuit!"

"Nothing . . . it's only . . . really nothing. So what did the client say then when you said if he didn't like the L'il P.T. nebbish idea he could . . . ?"

"Oh, no you don't, Biscuit! Look, I'm not going to tell you and Miss G. to see a gynecologist once more! I'm going to handcuff you both and drag you there on your asses!"

"Daddy, don't say asses. Say 'hineys' or 'fannies.' Kiss Miss Grumpet and make her well, Daddy."

Fortune had rung the doorbell then. She heard a sudden scuffling. A radio blared. Water began running. Campbell, rumpled, his hair in a cockatoo at the crown of his head as if it had, yes, been smashed on a pillow . . . he wore no shirt. How unsettling . . . his chest, his hair, his nipples, two angry little buttons. Gummy and cross, he had said, "Hi."

"I came about a costume," she said.

"You came about a costume," said Campbell.

Biscuit blew into view. She stopped to massage her temples. She carried a dust mop. "Daddy? Who is it? Why, it's Roomie! Of all people! How did you find us?"

"In *The Dionysus Dateline*." She remained standing on the WELCOME mat.

"You know I thought I heard someone's voice at the door . . . I was back here cleaning and cleaning. And, Daddy . . . you still here? I thought I sent you to buy me some Ajax!" To Fortune: "Sometimes boyfriends think girlfriends are only good for one thing—clean, clean, clean! Poor whales

34

and snails and puppy dogs' tails . . . what would they do without their 'womenfolk,' right, Roomie?"

The costume information was settled. Go to West Coast Costumery.

"I'll walk home with you, Roomie." Biscuit rattled some dustpans and trash cans. "You go ahead . . . I'll catch up with you. I want to finish something up."

Fortune walked across the courtyard again. Her high heels, pencil-thin, punched into the grass. She liked these extreme shoes . . . what if they *were* witchy and out-of-date! Spike heels—*her* shoe. Lovely . . . carries herself! Graceful . . . on those slender shoes. . . . The height of the shoes sometimes threw her off balance, but she did not lurch if she thought about it. She was thinking about it now. Who is that new girl? The mysterious one. . . .

The name of the place stood out on a stucco wall in large letters. Shrubbery lights flooded it. The calligraphic heads of palm trees dotted the *i*'s. VILLA DIONYSUS. Through these portals pass the swingingest singles on the face of the earth. Watch your step.

❀

Biscuit stripped nude in a flash. Fortune had no time to turn her eyes away. Biscuit was swift . . . then she flounced into bed nude. She tugged and patted, arranging her stuffed animals at her pillow. A griege elephant, "Barbar," went down under the sheets with her. Fortune had already begun to talk; she could not stop.

She had ducked into the bathroom to undress. She untangled her nightgown . . . she was talking, telling things, unimportant stories, gabbily, almost happily. She was relieved to be under a roof. Relief made her gabby. Biscuit's friendliness set her off . . . and so had the eavesdropping at Campbell's door . . . and earlier still, The Sugar Crumbs and Costumes Affair. And just now Biscuit's terse nudity made her talk and talk. Had she said she hoped Biscuit would show her the ropes about how a person was expected to act at Dionysus West?

She came out of the bathroom. Biscuit was sleeping. She lay very still beneath a sputtering snore. Disappointment lasted only for a moment . . . the new mauve peignoir, ostrich feathers at hem and throat, could be noticed tomorrow.

She went out and stood on the balcony, for anybody passing below in the driveway. People did go by, one, two. Someone spoke. "Oh, well, you know that old scene." It was a woman's voice from below, commenting in the dark. (*What* scene, Bert?) The balcony faced another Villa living room. Those curtains were open. The lights were on. There was no one there.

She lay and stared up into the dark. Biscuit's snore sounded like cards shuffled in a "no shit" (like they said) poker game. She stared out the window. She was frightened. She would have liked to masturbate. But Bert said: We thought you were giving that up when you got out to California, along with smoking! She did not answer him, the son of a bitch. He said: . . . new life out here! . . . And would you really call *that* turning over your best leaf forward?

*

She always awakened early . . . out of fear that the day would get the drop on her.

Biscuit was still a mound under striped sheets.

36

Fortune prepared for her debut . . . intricately . . . she studied her body . . . white as cheese.

Sunshine and bodies fanned out around the swimming pool, the bronzing Saturday action. Isolated heads bobbed on the water like heads served on a platter . . . a vast, cool, illusive plate. The sight transfixed her for a moment . . . those heads, that water. They ducked and dunked.

She stood at the Coca-Cola machine, faking dimes, doors. And she watched the Dionysids at the pool. They had tattoos, sideburns, chests and breasts; toothpicks stuck out of their mouths; and out of their hair, pencils. There were moles . . . scars, other imperfections. But, still, they handled their imperfect bodies with self-confidence. Now they flopped into the pool. Now they surfaced or leaned forward in their pool chairs. When they leaned forward, the skins of their backs bore the waffle-relief of the chaise longue. The smells . . . chlorine, suntan oil, hair spray . . . some girl squirted her hair with a can of Style. It all meant something. Fortune wore new sunglasses, feline. They were a good, dark mask. The mauve swimsuit had the little flare of pleats.

Impudent, miss, that bit of skirt you have thought to delight us with . . . us around the pool. You seem to be an individual a man cannot keep from sitting up . . . notice of! I like them "willowy" like you. A real individual.

Cleavage? She sucked in her stomach and hunched her shoulders together, and walked out from behind the Coca-Cola machine.

Will you tell the court what that first moment . . . all eyes turned?

She had made it to the chaise longue. Now she lay, eyes closed, slits. She could barely make out the placid rubber rafts. They floated by, these rafts, bearing their limp cargo that drank Bud from pop-top cans. She sat up and squirted herself with suntan lotion. She lay down again quickly and closed her eyes. Her heart felt like a cavalry charge . . . and she began to wonder why it was hell . . . why did human beings show each other their bodies in these rituals by seashores and poolsides? Clothes had been invented for a purpose. Out of kindness, consideration to the human eye of your neighbor. I, Bert, have always hated—yes, H-A-T-E— swimming pools and beaches. The bulges, the bulging crotches of men . . . and no matter how hard they tried, the women and their pubic feathers and the suits chafing, chafing. . . .

Someone dove into the pool. The stray rain landed on her chest. Her dark sunglasses . . . do you think our friend, the ostrich, Miss Dundy, fooled anybody in the sand? . . . did not cover her enough. Verily, verily we say unto you, you are like our friend the ostrich.

A half an hour passed.

Behind her eyelids dreams occurred and bright warring pinpoints of color. She strained to be anonymous. She heard things, as if she were blind. A wet towel slopped onto cement. Straps snapped. Chairs scraping. Voices . . . conversations. All around her the Saturday action talked, "shot the bull," and "bitched" and blended, sheathing her in it all.

"Hey, Milner . . . while you're up . . ."

"On the lift at Sun Valley . . . wouldn't throw away that spray can because I kind of like the way those fit your little . . ."

"Really fun person to get stoned with."

38

"Borrows it to vacuum his goddamn car!"

"Some kindergarten-primary job in Lemon Grove. . . ."

"So who needs that shuck, I ask you!"

"I wanted them, she didn't . . . two kids don't cramp her style?"

"Oh, he's a very, very together person."

"So I stuck it under M instead of Mc and you'd think I'd f***ed up his whole filing system . . ."

Beg pardon, miss? There was something about the way you came out from behind that Coca-Cola machine. Your eyelashes dropping down there kind of shy to watch your step and that little sass of a skirt flirting over your . . . "hiney." Do forgive our off-color! Once every six months. We get a little rough and masculine, male and merry when we get relaxed. And if you ask us, Miss Newaroundtown, relax! Move easy! That is our motto. Now *that* is complete dionyzation.

"Ask her if we can borrow a squirt of her Bain de Soleil. Her . . . her in the purple."

Beg pardon, miss? We have been watching you there for a while.

"Honey? Hey, excuse me, hey . . . ?"

Who is that mystery woman over there under the Foster-Grants? Hmmmm. I like them like that . . . you might say I like them skinny even. Hmmm, but how can we get her to take notice of us? I know! You pretend you want to borrow some of her Bain de Soleil!

"Say, hon, excuse me. Could we have a dab of your Bain de Soleil there? Hey . . . lady? Honey?"

She counted to ten and sat up. To pretend she had just

39

awakened from (a bower of) sleep. The man was not that close. But she could smell his man smell . . . his oil, his tobacco, his androgen rising out of his pores.

"Your Bain de Soleil there. Thanks." He squooshed her suntan cream onto his shins. "You're new around here, aren't you? Where you from?"

"Oh . . . hah hah haaargh! 'Out West' . . . 'Up North' . . . 'Down South' . . . 'Back home' . . . Mars—take your pick!" she said.

"Yep," he said.

She introduced herself. Still squooshing, the man shook her hand with his left. He thanked her for the cream. His name was Buzz, no last name. His friend, Ron, used the Bain de Soleil then. "Thanks," Ron said. "This is good stuff. You better be careful there yourself, sweetheart. Your chest is going to peel. Look like a potato chip. Can't get too much the first time."

"Oh, do I know!" Potato chip . . . her chest? "One time I was down here at Playa del Rey beach. There was a person with a wristwatch tattooed on his wrist after I ran into a man in tight pants in Hollywood. Oh, I would say it was a good three, four hours after that. I was planning to get to the beach before the sun went down. And what do you know? It had not gone down far enough but I had my knees burned, 'like potato chips,' like you say. You can never tell what the sun is going to do is my opinion on the subject."

Ron . . . fading, leaving, dimming . . . said, "Yeah, it can really get hot."

She reported to him on the sunburn, her "big burn of 1955." It cut her down with fever. It could have sent her to the hospital. There were sunburns known to do that. She told

Ron and Buzz what her burn had looked like . . . how long it took to heal and then how it looked after it had healed. Ron and Buzz dove into the pool.

She lay back on the chaise longue, quivering from effort.

Much later she rose and walked to the pool's edge. She sat down and dangled her feet in the water.

The tops of her thighs could fool a lot of people. When I am sitting, Bert, my legs look more like they should . . . plumped out this way. Hah, there were so many little ways! So many little ruses! So many things the world never knew about her.

All the women at the pool today did not look like secretaries. Some looked like princesses. Magic . . . with emphatic bodies. They lolled and sunned, undoing their straps. A person could, however, compete with them. If she kept her head about her. And used it.

But one girl—with breasts like impossible ideas—this girl swam with no bathing suit brassiere. She flipped and dove like a porpoise, a mermaid . . . and her breasts flashed in the sun. People watched her calmly. Soon the girl disappeared into an apartment.

What a show-off!

The thing to do, Bert, is be opposite. For example, sitting down now at the edge of the pool—that had been a blue-ribbon idea. A person could play toes with the water. She could turn her face sunward, stretch her throat up, up . . . pale sun goddess in mauve! Where did you come from, pale, pale goddess?

A horsey girl in a black tank suit swooped on the scene, rough as a lifeguard. She began to play in the shallow end, her broad brown shoulders wagging in the water. Ron and

Buzz bobbed up next to this girl. The three ducked and splashed, wiping their hands over their streaming faces. The girl did not seem to be wearing a bit of makeup. Oh, she surely did think she was "something on a stick" for sure, that girl; swimming around, having close-ups with the boys . . . no, Big Brown, we do *not* think you are Esther Williams.

An ambush occurred. A thrashing force pulled Fortune into the water by her ankles. She cried out. She clutched in panic at the pool's ledge. Away she went, underwater. She was drowning. She thrashed. From underneath, the water's surface glinted . . . a promised sky. She struggled to surface. She did, churning and gagging. Someone said, "Whoa! Sorry about that. Hold on there! You're okay. Put your feet down."

Ron stood there, waist-deep. He was scooping Kleenex tissues out of the water. He handed her the pulp. "You lose this just now?"

"NO!!! That is not mine!!!"

"You sure, honey? Take a look at the top of your swimsuit."

She lost her mind. She tried to hunch down in the water. *"Oh, this water does feel good!!! Oh yes—swim, swim, swim, just like a duck!"*

She dog-paddled frantically toward the steps. But she saw beyond all question of a doubt . . . the rest of her stuffing followed her, disintegrating from the top of her swimsuit like pastel seaweed.

Ron called after her: "Man, I'm sorry. Didn't mean to be so rough." He waded over to the pool's edge and slopped a handful of Kleenex pulp onto the tile.

4

It was like a murder, irretractable. It lay locked in despair's embrace . . . a memory cloud.

She is thinking all this but says nothing.

(Mrs. Shortt shuffles around her, sucking Vicks drops. She steps up, pins here, tucks there.) The costume is too large. But it is a good one. She is going as Uncle Sam—striped pants, silver lamé coattails, stylized stovepipe hat encrusted in silver glitter.

The waistband is too big. So is the crotch. Mrs. Shortt bastes and Fortune stands daydreaming.

When asked to dance, Bert, a person can do one of two things: smile, rise without a word, put your hand out and go on with him to the dance floor. Or you begin the conversation before arriving on the floor.

And from the wings: Who . . . is she? The one in silver? Blah blah whisper whisper psssss psssss.

Who am I? she says to the stag who cut in on her partner. Some call me . . . Fortunée.

She got on the bus. People stared at her. She paid no attention. "*. . . stand beside her and guide her to the land with the light from above,*" she sang quietly. Somehow—it was annoying the way crazy things happened when you were all dressed up—her unnaturally tall hat grazed the overhead bar. Glitter rained down on the Naugahyde bus seat and the patent leather purse of some woman. In small raindrop sounds.

The lady said, "Oh-oh!"

"Do you know who I am?" Fortune said. The lady's dress, polka dots, bothered her eyes.

"Uncle Sam?"

"On the nose!"

At Villa Dionysus she said to Biscuit and her boyfriend: "Do you think they'll like it?"

"Yes, it's very convincing," they answered.

"Yes, that is my opinion on it, too." She curled her eyelashes and watched Campbell through the eyelash curler. "The fellow at the West Coast Costumery told me all I have got to do is point my finger at any draft-age males at the party and say, 'I want you!' "

"Right on," Campbell said, "you'll be stampeded."

The Villa courtyard was splendid. Red-white-and-blue bunting hung everywhere . . . rails, buffet tables lined with lights.

Fortune sat with Biscuit and a brace of Dionysids . . . Corki, Laura, G.P., Harry, etc. Some crisp, "collegiate," perfectly preserved, the way they had left college years before. Crew cuts, "Princetons," Dinah Shore do's side by side with Afros and Ho Chi Minh chins and so on. And these last ones, timidly funky, not quite Aquarian but, rather, middle-brow with token patches on their asses . . . a flag, a strawberry. Nowhere could she see the evil Ron of . . . The Kleenex Affair.

Girls in bikinis sat on some men's laps. Other men snapped wet towels at the passing, jouncing buttocks of other girls. Someone unfurled a woman in an American flag . . . into the pool. The water was a mad froth of people and battles. There were strobe lights on the balcony, grinding out color . . . they painted the pool in colored light, it floated like scarves on the water. Had the girl in the flag been naked? Yes . . . but she disappeared. Why is it naked women appear and disappear . . . ? Who can say? The strobe light on the water was beautiful, crazy.

Campbell arrived. The man named Harry hissed and laughed, jumping up to ghost-spar with him. They cuffed and sniffed and jabbed at each other. Campbell was wearing the Farmer John bib overalls, the Li'l Abner boots. The people at the table were calling him the Secretary of Agriculture. Someone then said Biscuit was the Farmer's Daughter. "Hi, Daddy! Hi, Daddy!" Biscuit had said. "Let's go swimming, Daddy! Where's your trunks?"

"Hey, come on, Biscuit," someone said. "We know you know where the Secretary of Agriculture last dropped his trunks!"

Biscuit froze. She rose, gave the speaker a look—"to melt stone," Bert—and ran away. Campbell ran after her. Fortune could see them, hear them. They stood together in the door of the recreation hall, forehead to forehead. Biscuit chewed on the corner of her farmer-wife apron. Her face was tragic.

"He was only trying to be funny," Campbell said.

"You know what he was trying to insinuate!" said Biscuit. Then the pile-driving music started, "Proud Mary." The band called themselves No Return. The catatonic music buried everything. Campbell put his nose to Biscuit's and wiggle-waggled it. Biscuit doubled over. Fortune recognized this—it was the pain movement, Miss Grumpet.

"That's some costume Roomie has, isn't it, Harry?" Biscuit said when they came back.

"Yes," said Harry, rolling up a pack of Lucky Strikes in the sleeve of his T-shirt, "Uncle Sam if I ever saw him." Harry was watching a girl climb out of the pool. She shook like a spaniel and squeezed water out of her wet ropes of hair. She hitched at the straps of her swimsuit and tucked her escaping thighs back up into it. "This your first ordeal, Sam?"

"Yes, it is, Harry. And yourself there?"

"Oh no. I've been around a while."

"And yourself, Harry. What sort of a profession do you do? You must do something that you use your arms and shoulders a lot. *Proud Mary, keep on . . . Left a good job . . .*"

"I'm out at Sears. Photography department."

"Try a Vogue?" The strobe light passed over her. Grains of reflected light from her hat fell upon the wet tile.

"Harry, I told Roomie you'd show her the slides from the April Fool party. Is the slide room locked? Find Tuck. Bye! We're going to dance one quickie and then change into our suits." Biscuit led Campbell out onto the tennis courts. There they jumped and gyrated, simulating the dance steps of other, slightly younger Dionysids with better senses of rhythm.

"Aw, swing it!!!" Fortune shouted to them. She flicked her

46

Vogue, tapped her foot and hummed. "This music has got real zip," she said to Harry, offering him a Vogue again.

"No," he said politely. "No, thank you. I have my brand."

❀

Do not lie to me, Bert! I am not lying, Miss Dundy, our judges *have* been able to come up with a Date for you, I am talking as straightforward as the nose on the back of your hand. A Date coming up at 4:00 this A.M. July Five you have got a D-A-T-E, date! If you are lying to me, Bert, I will kill you.

He had medical-looking hands. She knew it the moment she had laid eyes on them. Hands were one thing she knew.

"I met a dentist. Dr. Samuel Fritchey," she told Biscuit.

"What??? Here? At this party? They invited *him*? They invited Skip Fritchey?"

"No. He was cutting across to his car. He left something in his office. It's downstairs in A Wing."

"Well, well! Isn't that nice that with all these men at this nice party you stumbled across Skip Fritchey and he stumbled across you? Isn't that nice?"

"Yes, it is nice," said Fortune. To "put it mildly," Bert.

"Isn't that nice, Daddy?"

"Shee-yit," her boyfriend said to this.

"Daddy, bad talk! Anyway, she's not particular, are you, Roomie?"

"Beg pardon?" (Yes, Bert, a person could be said to be particular.)

Campbell reminded Biscuit of "that Mother's Day Dance. He gate-crashed that one, too." It seemed that at that dance

Fritchey had drawn Campbell aside. He had pointed out various women there who he thought would be "the best ones to plug." The dentist had added that a man should find out which were divorcées, they were always the horniest. Later Campbell danced with Biscuit. "We met at that dance, remember?" The dentist, according to Campbell, would walk back and forth then and wink at Campbell . . . because of Biscuit. "I swear that bastard was winking at me!"

Biscuit looked uncomfortable. She smiled sickly and turned her face away. Through her teeth: "Drop the subject, will you?" Then, loudly: "Daddy, Roomie here is going to think you and Skip are just a pair of nasty, rasty men! Right, Roomie?"

"Beg pardon?"

"Plug!" Campbell cried. He skidded on a watermelon rind. "Plug! Let him! Crasty bastard! Let him!" He pulled away from Biscuit's restraining finger; she was trying shakily, jocularly, to touch his lips, shush, shush. "Plug! Let him hump, screw, jazz, ball, hose, bang . . . !"

"Daddy," Biscuit begged in agony, ". . . someone's going to hear you."

Plug. Plllllllllug. Too late. The word had attached itself to Fortune's thoughts. It clung there like a cocklebur to a sock.

"I don't give a rat's ass *who* hears me! Someday I'm going to knock that bastard's teeth so far down his throat he'll be farting fillings!"

"DADDY! *I will not, no, I will NOT put up with that language!*"

They left.

Later, much later, when things were ending, Fortune raced to B-12. She still had no key. She rang the bell.

"Minute!" called Biscuit. "Shampoo in my eyes!"

She opened the door unpleasantly, a towel wrapped around her head.

"I won!" Fortune cried. "I won!"

"Roomie! Why, it's my old Roomie at the door! Oh, and you *did* win. So they had the judging after all! We heard a rumor they were calling off the . . . we were up here putting our swimsuits on! And the closet door, Milo's fixing that. And so you won! Why, sure . . . and there you have your trophy! Well, if we can pull Milo away from that repair job long enough, he'll certainly share our joy! Daddy! Oh, Daddy!"

Fortune pressed her face into the space Biscuit left open at the door. "Harry said I should show you my trophy."

"And it's beautiful, Roomie, it certainly is!"

"But you should see it under the light."

"Oh, we can! It's great!"

"I want to come in. I want to get my Brownie flash out of the drawer to get a snap of myself with the trophy. I will be in the *Dateline* and the *Grapevine*, they told me. I have got to turn in a picture. I feel bad your nice costumes did not get a chance. I wanted to find you first. But it happened too fast. 'Like quicksilver.' I want to come in. Can I come in?"

She had gone to her new apartment. And the two of them, her roommate and the roommate's boyfriend, two people with genitals, had been in the dark apartment. How did you know, Miss Dundy, at that time . . . ? Because the bedclothing was a big lie.

All the lights were out, except those on the name, VILLA DIONYSUS. Two couples remained in the chaise longues, kiss-

49

ing, talking. Red and blue crepe-paper streamers bled onto the tile around the still swimming pool. Watermelon rinds floated there. Occasionally she stepped on an olive pit, a celery stick. A glass broke somewhere in an apartment. Someone called, ". . . it tomorrow!" Cars honked, doors slammed, and a stereo throbbed. Fortune tried not to think about the dentist; she was trying not to jinx him.

Someone came by. A girl . . . leaving, perhaps arriving. Fortune asked her to take a picture. And the girl did and wandered on, very drunk, into the breezeway. She passed under the giant American flag fluttering down by an unattached corner.

But you did take notice of their behavior that was afoot . . . the dentist . . . same thing to you?

". . . stand beside her and guide her to the land . . ."

You going to sing, Miss Dundy . . . or cooperate? See your blah blah at least blah blah this: Was there this so-called pl****** atmosphere in the air when blah blah . . . ?

Stop! Yes, all right, I said it!

Raise your right hand and repeat after me, please: P . . . L . . . U . . . G. Now, step blah blah isolation booth and read aloud this newspaper classified, please.

Hands Across the Sea: Pen Pals Intn'l. For list, L.A. Free Press

---

LITHE BOY Scorpio longs to be whipped

Girls: Find Out Is Myth True Call Stud Sambo Hurry While I Last

MARRIED couple with bag of tricks looking for same for weekends

---

SAM THE MAN: Dentist's Delight: Erotica Stainless Steel Probes Picks Pliers Plugs Come One Come All You Will All Come.

5

She wrote a letter to the lovelorn column of the *Grapevine*,
a corner called "Hung-Up" in the weekly flyer-newspaper.

"Dear 'Miss Ima Shoulder' I am a new gal Dionysid and
I am wondering advice about the subject of 'crossed wires'
when a man says I will meet you by the swimming pool at
four A.M. and then he does not this is not a true story in this
letter it is just a question I have got about a person I know
my sister let us say that had a date and the man said meet
me at such and such and then he got 'wires crossed' or he
got in a car wreck on these freeways we have got in this
state do not get me wrong I love Calif. they surely did 'break
the mold' in making it does he really mean I will call you
and what you thought he says is I will meet you a long time
ago my sister let us say met somebody in checkered pants
that said I will call you and she this person was standing near
the front door of the Elks Hall Ballroom and looked like 'a
million dollars' she wore mauve that was her color and people told her stick with that color and you will go a long way
she was twenty-one years old and her girlfriend was dancing
the whole night with a poor person that had an Adam's apple the size of your fist that is too bad men should get oper-
ated on and a hand-tooled belt with his name on it Gideon

and the man the person in mauve picked out though he had
a sly way I liked he just stood there not looking at me just
smoking and polishing his toe it was an alligator shoe up
against his pants legs I have always had an eye for those
people of this world that are something more than just your
everyday of the mill person she asked the man did he beg
pardon have the time of day would you be so kind to tell a
young lady it on your wristwatch and he said he did not
wear one oh beg pardon she said back to him at that time
he did not say another word the next ten minutes she said
okay excuse me and she went to the powder room not to
blot her lipstick on the walls the way the trashy women do
and she fixed her corsage she always wore one fresh on her
wrist and to check her makeup and give him outside time
to think her over later she went and stood by him and she
sang along with the band she can really sing it was a 'cat'
song like they said in those days by Bill Haley and the
Comets if you remember them they are not like the music of
today but she sure could sing and so she sang along about
thirteen women and Bill the only man in town she smoked
too that is always a good thing to do if he is smoking then
he lights yours that is a tip I can pass on to you Miss Shoulder for our readers the mauve gown was chiffon from a wedding the fall before there was a punch stain on the skirt but
if a person is clever she hides the stain in the folds if she
keeps swishing around I will call you and you and me will
go out tomorrow he said that do not think Miss Shoulder he
did not have class because of his grammar faults we all in
this world are not perfect not even you then in the car out
in the parking lot of that old Elks Hall a wonderful place
that is standing no more but I 'remember it well' like they

53

say he wanted to kiss and his lips went clamp over my mouth a snail on a fish bowl meanwhile there he went that was a 'mean disappointment' he was wanting to touch my 'privates' just my chest to 'pet' is the best word and he smashed my corsage I was sad and I am sorry he did do that What about going back inside my sister says then but checker britches says I do not know how to dance that is okay I will show you she says and she did one-two push my rib now turn is the easiest way to show a beginner and she sure could dance she is known for her dancing and could go professional ask anybody that sees her I will call you was what the man said then okay all the next day Sunday she goes to wait at her girlfriend's house the one with the telephone because Sook's mother and her sister 'with child' and the sister's three children all went to Word of Light in the morning and to family for supper and they were gone and she my friend that had the telephone that had the date with the alligator shoes person waits at the telephone she did her hair and her nails and finally took her bath even though she left the bathroom door open to hear better it sounded like ringing but it never was and she did not splash or make noise and she knew that a watched pot never boils so she promised no she would not look at that telephone you can jinx things by doing that the day goes by and goes by and she tries not to think but instead she sits in the bedroom on the bed and draws pictures on a brown paper bag one side of the bag she makes a landscape drawing pointed trees with a girl sitting by a river she wears a crown playing a guitar and on the other side of this bag she draws eyebrow shapes some closed with lashes do you know how Sunday sounds so quiet it is you hate it so quiet you think you can hear the leaves outside rusting and rotting on the ground like they are talking to you and the old rainwater in the tire shell in the backyard do not ask me if he called you can guess by now and even the bulbs underground talk it is that quiet do not think there is something wrong with yours truly I do not really hear dead things talk I only was wondering if you could help with the problem of why men say one thing and do another thing to

"The Lady in Lavender."

She stood on the balcony. A listless breeze caught the hem of the peignoir. She had been watching a man on an apartment balcony across the way. Bare-chested, he ate donuts. His eyes were closed. Once in a while he would open his eyes and flick sugar flakes off his chest.

The doorbell brayed suddenly. She flew into the bathroom and tried to glue on her eyelashes. Not knowing who it was but certain it was the dentist. Even now at eleven-thirty Sunday morning. It was Campbell, sluggish and barefoot; he came for the Sunday *Times.*

Biscuit was still sleeping, she told him. No, don't wake her up! he cried; she's tuckered out!

Coffee? Tea? Sanka? Tang? Did he want anything?

"Yeah. You can lay a little coffee on me." He read the *Times,* all over the couch.

Fortune began to brush her hair. She sat at the table and lighted a dead half-smoked Vogue. She went through the classified, whispering aloud to herself. "Now . . . let us see, let us see . . . *Keypunch,* no . . . *PBX,* no . . . ah, here is one, *'Attractive . . .'* "

"We didn't know you were job-hunting." Campbell lifted his head.

". . . and *'Discount King needs exp. woman public relations.'* Hmmmm . . . I do not know about . . . 'Discount King?' What sort place is that? 'Discount King.' That 'discount' part has got a peculiar buzz to it . . . sounds common. And keypunch! Keypunch, they all want keypunch! Ah . . . *'Photographer's model'!*"

Biscuit shuffled in, scratching at her shorty pajamas. She and the stuffed elephant fell upon Campbell. Biscuit nuzzled his neck, her eyes closed. He hugged her. He called her his "sleepy-time gal." Biscuit, eyes closed, trancelike, worked her mouth in and out, like a nursing calf. She clucked it wetly once and fell silent again, pretending she was asleep.

Campbell whispered, "What kind of work you looking for?"

Fortune, by this time, was on the balcony. "Beg pardon?" She told him she was not interested in just any sort of "bread-and-butter" position; she wanted something where she could "meet the public on its own terms."

Biscuit leaped up. "Whuh? Where am I? Me dreamum! Oh, Daddy, you're here!" She hugged Campbell. "Me was having ugly dream, Daddy. Me dream her over thereum said she no have got job. But me know that not true because me knowed she knowed how much the rent costs. Plenty. Oh, me so glad it all a dream, Daddy!" She fell back again, pretending to sleep. Then she blinked, "Wake-um-upping," and sat up. "Good morning, everybody. How'd I get in here? Hello, Roomie. And how was your date with Skip Fritchey?"

She lay on the bed, with the classified ads. She could hear them fixing lunch. Whack! went the breadboard. Bang! the cupboard door.

"You heard her," Campbell said. "Public relations."

"Public relations!" Whack! "Public relations. Oh. Well, more power to them that's got it. More power to her."

"Now, don't get upset, honey, you'll have Miss G. . . ."

"What I don't understand is why she doesn't run for Rose Bowl Princess!!! Or the Senate!"

"Now, honey," he said.

"Gimme kiss."

Fortune peeked.

They were just now drawing apart from the kiss. Biscuit stared into Campbell's eyes. She wore a small, occult smile; her eyes were glittering like the taillights of a sports car. Glistening nefariously on her bottom lip was a single drop of blood. Macabre. *"Un-cle,"* she said languidly, staring into his eyes. Out came her cryptic tongue then and, like a reptile's, flicked the blood away.

Campbell turned away.

Fortune pulled back and leaped onto her bed. Then she heard Campbell say for Biscuit not to hit him in the face, Beverly, he did not like it, Biscuit, to be hit in the face.

"What'samatta, Daddy? My big Daddy going soft on his little girl?"

"You don't hit a man in the face. Men don't like that. Even in play."

Fortune was breathing as if she would burst. She laid her cheek against the wall. Once again she made her way to the crack at the door . . . and peeped. Campbell stood holding

Biscuit's wrists clamped in his hand—he was a big man, it was now apparent—and he raised his other hand as if to strike her. Then Biscuit pretended "uncle." When Campbell released her, she feinted, and with a little capriole, slapped him soundly across the face. Spinning off, she said, "If it's one thing for people to be when they're job-hunting, that thing is realistic." She grabbed the bread knife and hurled it at the bedroom door. "You asleep, Roomie?"

No, a person could not be said to have been *asleep*, exactly. But not exactly *awake*, either. And about that Bread Knife Affair: if people get *too* fancy, the *other* person would have to open her purse. You see, Miss Dundy does happen to carry, Your Honor, a . . . kitchen knife of her own in her purse to sharpen her pencils and when she never knows walking in some parts of this City of Angels when . . . waltz up behind her in the night like happened to that girl found in the garbage cans off Severance Street. Pencils or people in the night—Miss Besqueth should "think twice" about Bread Knives Against Bedroom Doors. Oh, Bert, you "overreact on molehills" sometimes. I was only meaning "a word to the wise" to her. But, yes, and this purse here of mine the court sees before you *is* see-through. I will leave it around B-12 sometime. I will even leave it open sometime . . . "casual." She will see. There will be no need for words. Fortune smoked and fanned. With her Japanese fan, every evening now she sat by the pool. People . . . coming, going. She watched apartment doors. One would open from time to time and chuck another Dionysid. Fortune would count the door and look it up in the *Dateline*. . . . Who lives there? Who was that apartment door all about? A stranger is just a friend she hah-hah had not tracked down in the *Dateline* yet! Maybe with *your* black magic and *my* spell . . . ! But she was waiting for the dentist. His office had been dark for nine days now. She had once said to Biscuit: "Do you think that that dentist got in a car wreck?"

"Who?" Biscuit had been at the closet, doing something to a dress.

"Dr. Fritchey."

"Had an accident? What! Is he all right!!!"

"No. I say, do you suppose he might have had some little car crack-up?"

"When?"

"The other night. That night."

"What night?"

"The Fourth of July celebration."

"Christ-o, what are you talking about?"

"When he did not show. Maybe he was hurt on some freeway and afraid to tell me later."

"Forget it."

"Beg pardon?"

"He just didn't come. Men sometimes don't," Biscuit said.

Men sometimes do not come. That was the same advice "Miss Ima Shoulder" gave back in the *Grapevine*. At the bottom of the column—the others were short, silly letters about arguments with boyfriends—she had made a note: *To "The Lady in Lavender": Your letter was too long to run, although it was quite a work of art. But here's a tip: get hip.* And then the part about men sometimes do not come.

"Oh, yes he does come!" Fortune had said to Biscuit. "Or he has got himself a real reason!"

"Puh-leez duh-rop it. Besides, I forbid you to mention his

name in this house. Zip me up, will you? Thank you. Now, to me, a place like, say, Van de Kamp's sounds like lots of fun! And tips galore!"

"Thank you, too, for your interest, but I have not got waitress work in mind."

✿

"Work for my woman, toil for my kids, sweat like the devil all the day . . . !" She had gotten a job. She would begin demonstrating cake-decoration guns on the mall at a shopping center in Westwood. They would pay her an hourly wage. She would earn a commission for every decorating set she sold. She told Biscuit and Campbell that if the world was not careful cake decorating as an art would soon disappear. "Have you ever seen these one-squirt throw-away cartridges the supermarkets are trying to push off on the public? Those serve-ur-self racks? Why, they no more give a person a chance to make a cake a refined thing . . . than if you told a doctor, 'Doctor, do this heart transplant with these hedge clippers.' But now, you take a look at us!"

She demonstrated on the underside of an enamel dishpan. "On the job, I use real cakes and demonstrate the sidelights on this pan, my 'demonstrating pan.' Then I can erase if I want to. See here—swirling motion with the wrist gives you your rose! An up-and-down rhythm and you have got your zigzag . . . and stop it a second and there you have got a carnation! Fancilize the edge here with your loop-the-loop. And for a change of tune . . . oh-oh . . . well, every so often you have got yourself a dot-dot-dash (we could call that your 'Morse code trim,' could we not? Hah hah hah hah!) . . . and you are on your way with Deco-Cake! How

60

do we make rosebuds? you ask. I will show you. We make rosebuds with a . . . one little base like that . . . smaller squish just so . . . end up in your little bud! Looks like she is about to open, does she not? Let us say you are in the market to use another color, you just slip your nozzle onto your cloth frosting gun here, squeeze like this here, gentle, gentle with the palm of the hand—the secret of success is in the palm pressure—and there you go, simple as taking pie from a baby. Now: you ask me, what about stars, Miss Dundy? Why, you just slip on your Star Nozzle! Watch close. And has Deco-Cake got other nozzles? We surely do. Take a look for yourself, do not take my word . . . not one or two or three but four different nozzles. Giving you your various frosting flows and shapes. Now: you say to me, 'Miss Dundy, all this is real "well and good," like they say, and I even think I could decorate a little cake at home, Miss Dundy, but would I be wrong, Miss Dundy, in trying, say, a *wedding cake?*' No, friend, you would not. I am mistaken or you are all saying to yourself right now, 'But how?' How? I am going to show you. For only a few little round and rolling copper centavos more, we will throw in for you our special Wedding Nozzle.

"There she is! Makes not one, not two, but three different designs for that very special event when those bells are going up in that steeple. You have got your . . . now watch close here . . . your Nuptial Rosette. That is with the nozzle straight up and down. And then you have got your formal ivy leaf. And we do hope you will be using white frosting. And then when you slant your nozzle like this, you have got what I like to call your Bridal Bordertrim. Now, a lady came in here the other day saying that is all 'well and good' if you have got the money. But hold your team, I told her, hold on while I tell you the price. This little extra Deco-Cake Wedding Nozzle is only—hold onto your hats—three quarters, shiny or dull, of an American dollar, plus four coppers. Yes, seventy-nine cents and we will throw in the Wedding Nozzle along with the rest! Well . . . I am going to tell you what that Doubting Thomasina did: she bought three Deco-Cake sets, three regular sets *plus* three Wedding Nozzles!"

❀

She wrote the *Dateline* to put a new blurb under her photograph: Professional Designer, Pastry. She put a card on the bulletin board in the rec hall. She was volunteering; she was free to anyone who showed her Dionysus West, Inc., identification. Someone called her. His name was Tucker Hadiman. He managed Dionysus West. He was recruiting volunteers for "The Steering Committee," a small body of "representatives from each wing. We're trying to upgrade the quality of life around here. I can't do it all by myself." Tucker had seen her card on the bulletin board. He thought she sounded like "a worker." Would she like to represent B Wing?

❀

"LET'S GET OUR SHIT TOGETHER NOW, LADIES!" Tucker clapped his hands.

Pretzels, gossip, cigarette smoke, six women and Tucker . . . his face soft, pouchy . . . eunuch's padding on the cheekbones, two little sandbars on his cheeks, eroded, abandoned there in the stream of his face. "The Bitch Board," that was what they called themselves, what Tucker called them all. The ants and the grasshoppers! The grasshoppers —the lazy asses of the club! The ants? Here, now, today!

"Right on, Tuck!" the women shouted.

The other "reps" handed in their complaints to Tucker, talking, smoking . . . problems all over the place. Where was "Turk" Mosallem, the big boss who owned DW and all the cousin clubs in San Francisco, Chicago, Phoenix . . . ? Where was the Big M?

"Calm down, people!" Tucker smoked Salems, called them candy sticks, took notes, promised to write T.M. "Doris, take this down: 'Dear Mr. Mosallem: Our apartment, D-9, Villa Dionysus, DW, Los Angeles, was burglarized last month. We would like your insurance agent in L.A. to contact us. . . .' And so on, Doris, wing it on out. Sign it Clancey Tinney and Mitzy Mips."

Tucker sighed. He brushed at his hair with a palm. "I mean, look, kids. This place can either be a bunch of people living in a bunch of apartments, wandering around like fraternity kids lost in the woods at a beer-bust—or it can be a real smash! It can move! It can say things! *We can even get into politics! Did that ever occur to you! Right! Mosallem for Congress! That day could come! You for Congress! Me for Congress! Fortunée Dundy for Congress! Here she is— our new little member! Meet the Bitch Board, Fortunée! Raaaaaaaaaaaaaaaay! Give her a hand!"*

A suggestion box! One for every wing . . . plans! And beer cans—what would they do about the beer cans left around the swimming pool? "Glenda!" Tucker cried. "Ditto off flyers! About the cans. You know, 'For the good of all . . . ,' that kind of thing. Next complaint!"

"Do I send it to his secretary or to him?" Doris asked.

"To Mosallem! Straight to him! No bureaucracy! Put 'Tony'—and in parentheses, ' "Turk" Mosallem'—'di Mossallini' on the envelope. It's some San Francisco address the Mob keeps . . . Montgomery Street or something . . . get the number in my office . . . don't get too free with the postage meter. Next!"

And so it went . . . everybody was complaining. The "reps" had had their noses in the wind . . . complaints about pets, dog droppings on the grass, failed air conditioning, noise, too much noise. (And somewhere in there Tucker interrupted: "Roger *Tway* said that? Roger Tway lives in Pacific Palisades! Ever notice how it's invariably Dionysids who live *outside* the Villa who bitch the most. The cop-outs. I mean, you know, Roger Tway himself is Geographically Undesirable, if you want to look at it that way. Oh, these commuters, these satellite people, they think they're so coy living out—and then they come to me with their 'lack of unity' rip-off.") And . . . complaints about the laundry room and then about the parties, caterers' shitty food. A woman in braids, a woman with all the wrong sort of face for braids, stood up and read from her spiral notebook. She kept notes. ("Beautiful," Tucker said. "Beautiful. Now, *that*, people, is what I call initiative.") The woman, Marilu, read: " 'The food is shitty at these parties. And with the dues they charge around this hole . . .' This is unsigned, I overheard it in the rec hall. '. . . this hole. So Hadiman can bring in sawdust and spread it on bread and call it a catered picnic lunch? Don't jack me.' "

Tucker had been sitting on the floor. Now he sprang up like a kangaroo rat. He slapped his Magic Marker on the coffee table and whipped his hair out of his eyes. "Oh, so they think I can be Boy Wonder and a f***ing Refreshments Chairman all rolled into one!!! But . . . wait a f***ing minute, people, wait a minute. I'm sorry. We won't fight them. We will not fight them. If they want better f***ing food, they will get better f***ing food."

"Right on, Tuck! Right on!"

Tucker stabbed the Magic Marker in the air. He trembled. He crouched. He whirled. "People, we'll honk on! Gastronomy from here on out! We'll make the Cordon Bleu taste like Howard Johnson's! You, Judy! You can be my big gun in this bitch! You hassle the caterers, you're right up front in knowing how to milk. . . . I'll take you to the office after the meeting, give you the food folder. Are you on?"

"I'm on, Tuck."

"Angel, I love you. People, I can write every f***ing inch of the *Grapevine* copy, the *Dateline* copy, I can hassle the DataMate office downtown translating computer clients into Dionysids, I can pay the f***ing musicians, keep the f***ing boutique stocked, negotiate with the f***ing gardeners, call the f***ing washing-machine repair place, see that the f***ing Friday night films in the rec hall aren't blurry, replace the f***ing dented Ping-Pong balls, chlorinate the f***ing pool–ah, not too much, not too little, that's my job!–arrange the f***ing moonlight hayrides down to the last f***ing horse, charter buses, balance the books–and still manage to catch between three and four hours' sleep a night! But, people, I cannot and will not send myself into a doctor's care for 'sawdust on sandwich bread,' for f***ing Clancey Tinney, f***ing Mitzy Mips, f***ing Roger Tway, *or* f***ing 'Turk' Mosallem!!!"

"RIGHT ON!"

"You tell them, Tuck!"

Then someone said, "Still, I don't know why when the caterers say 'catered picnic,' they can't send fried chicken and fruit and things like that. . . ."

"Not everyone in the club likes fried chicken."

"Who doesn't like fried chicken, my God? My God, everybody likes fried chicken. You're not going to have them bitching about the food if you give people fried chicken. . . ."

"This is getting nowhere, people. Let them eat fried chicken and shut up."

"I, for one, can think of more imaginative food than cold fried chicken on a picnic. If it's hot chicken, fully cooked, once in a while, it's good."

"Then it's not a picnic. All that cooking. Right there on the picnic site . . . frying chicken?"

"Fine, then it's not a picnic. But who wants cold, half-cooked pink tendons hanging out of a drumstick? I can think of more appetizing food than . . ."

"Name one."

"A big Virginia ham."

"Then you've got the Catholics to worry about if it's Friday."

"Or the Jews if it's not Friday."

"WILL YOU SHUT YOUR F***ING MOUTHS!" Tucker hurled his papers in the air. "All we're trying to do is make people happy in this club! Should that be so hard to do?"

"Just no uncooked tendons."

Tucker sank to the floor and lay there motionless, his eyes closed . . . thin parchment shades. Then reborn, he glanced up. The meeting continued. Donna Williams read her report. Fortune knew her from the laundry room; the *Grapevine* said she was engaged to "the boy back home" (Blythe, California), someone named Howard Goldfinger, who also had moved to Los Angeles but had "refused" to join Dionysus West. "This is from E-33. 'Tell Big Mosallem and his construction company next time try plaster instead of paper when they are jerry-building a Villa . . . five months and not one night have the heads in E-34 next door to me had the stereo off before two A.M. Normal working people sleep those hours, I don't know about the crash pad next door.' They would appreciate it, Tucker, if you would take some steps about the stereo."

"Didn't you, Donna, approach them yourself? What'd they say?"

"They said, 'F*** off.' "

Tucker sighed, made a note. Reports followed: . . . cockroaches coming up drains, laundry stolen out of dryers, newspapers "borrowed" off doorsteps, parking slots infringed upon by visitors . . . and again, thin walls.

Fortune's head ached. She sat, mesmerized, holding a pretzel. *Killer Phrase!* She had been wanting to shout this, for fun.

More gossip . . . somebody named Jeanine. Tucker chuckled and studied his cuticle. How cool he was! How adroitly he sidestepped the mess of other people's sorrows! He had no use for their chaos! Fortune was lulled; the sound of their pleasant, mesmerizing gossip almost caused her to miss a story with Biscuit's name.

. . . an account of Biscuit Besqueth's "f***ed-up id."

Someone on the Bitch Board used to live in an adjoining apartment. How Biscuit used to beg ". . . him to work her over. Wow. You know? Otherwise, she's okay."

(Thin walls: all this began because somebody had said "thin walls" again.)

And somebody else said, ". . . used to be married to that dentist downstairs. The guy with the office next to the boutique."

"Do I know?" hooted Tucker. "People, do *I* know!"

Tucker had rented Samuel Fritchey the office space. And a year ago he had turned Beverly Besqueth on to Dionysus West. He had known both people in a former life. "Do *I* know Biscuit Besqueth? Hah!" Tucker looked at his cigarette and put his finger over a wound in the paper to smoke. His family and hers were next-door neighbors in San Marino. As a child, Biscuit had been a little Shirley Temple of a thing. Then Tucker went away to Orme Ranch, a private school in Arizona. One Christmas vacation his mother said Biscuit had married some high-school boy. ". . . lasted about two months or something. Very *misterioso*. Biscuit miscarried. I don't know, man. Far be it from me to understand those people and their wild hairs." . . . he went on, in clumps of bored, detached biography.

". . . and I don't hold a drinking glass up to the wall, either!"

". . . have you rapped to them about it?"

"Come *on*, Tucker. What do I do—knock on the door and say, 'Look, neighbor, mind holding down the humping a little?' "

"It's the walls," someone said.

"Them's the breaks," said Tucker. "People who want

68

soundproofing better move to their own little isle in the Pacific. Society is what it is and noise is a by-product. Look, people, you have to learn to live with the grain of things. If there's so f***ing much they don't dig about this club, you know, love it or leave it. There are still over two thousand of us who can stay around and avoid middle age gracefully."

6

She was standing on the balcony. The man, Mr. C Wing Balcony, was out watering, yes, watering, Bert, his potted cactus. She had sold fourteen Deco-Cake sets today and was waiting for him to look up and read this success in her eyes.

She called over her shoulder, into the apartment . . . off-handedly, ah, what a casual note: "Am I mistaking? Or was that person you told me about in Newberry's . . . was he of the dentistry profession?"

Biscuit walked into view. Curler picks bristled from her teeth. She spit the picks onto the carpet to speak. "You try-ing to be cute or something?"

"Beg pardon?"

"Repeat the question. Only don't mention the bastard's name."

"What for have I got to repeat the question?"

"Oh, Christ-o. All right, so okay, so big deal! So I used to be married to him once upon a time the summer after high school! So you dug that up without much digging, so okay, so you can have him, so don't get up tight, all right?" (She stoops, straightens now. In her hand are the curler picks. She puts them back in her mouth and returns to the bathroom and goes on setting her hair. Fortune has followed her, says nothing.)

"Got me?"

"Yes. That is all right with me if you are asking my opinion on the subject. But he is not so much as a mustard seed to me if that is what you are 'up in the air about'!"

"Then let's drop it."

Fortune went back out onto the balcony to anneal.

From the bathroom Biscuit called: "Hey! One more little thing. Who told you?"

"A person."

"Terrifo. Christ-o. I don't give a shit who told you! Don't tell me. I won't let you tell me! Everybody knows—what the shit do I care? It's no big history, no big cross. Christ-o, half the people in this club are divorced! So I'm supposed to be all bent out of shape because you uncover I was once the Bride of Frankenstein? Divorce is *rare*, I suppose? It happens to the best and most all-together people. Divorce is not a big stigma . . . or . . . or some admission of failure, Christ-o. It's an agreement not to be married anymore. Marriage is a gamble. Divorce means odds were against you that time around. That is all divorce is. Nothing more! So don't act as if the sky is falling in, Chicken Little! I mean, the least little thing that happens to you, you always act like the sky's falling on your head!" She then came out on the balcony and said quietly, "So who told you?"

"A person that goes by the name of Tucker Hadiman."

"The little prick. I thought so, you going to that phoney meeting and all."

"I would not in my opinion say it is so . . . 'phoney'! If

it was not for him and us and some other ants, you grass-hoppers would not be so happy around here with things running smooth and things of that nature! I mean, come on, people."

7

Biscuit and Campbell walked into B-12 in the middle of the afternoon and found her on the balcony.

"Roomie, love!" cried Biscuit. "Home early? Thought you'd be at work." Campbell was carrying a small, rickety table. He set it down and blew some dust off it.

"No," Fortune said. She did not turn from the balcony, but continued staring out toward the freeway, turning the cigarette between her thumb and forefinger slowly. "No."

"Sick?" Biscuit said.

"Sick?" Now she turned her head and greeted them both solemnly and commented on their Salvation Army purchases. She turned back to gaze from the balcony again. "Yes, a person might say she is sick. Sick of people that will not leave a person to work up to their full talent."

"Oh, Christ-o, what is it now? You tell me, Daddy."

Fortune said then that if the world was not careful, real cake decorating was going to disappear. "When a person thinks about the binds they are putting on the profession."

"What, Fortunée, what, what?" Biscuit said.

"I was given a choice. I made it. And I told them why and they can put that in their pipe. My, look at that sky . . . those are some jet planes 'to remember.'"

A California health law said if you work around food, you must not have hair touching the collar; short hair . . . or you must wear a hairnet. "Cut this? I told my employer I happen to be an individual that's hair—we all remember Samson—is her glory. And talking about hairnets, I told him that is for fry cooks and carhops. How they hold the opinion that a person can meet the public on her own terms and its terms with all the hobbles they put on the profession I would be interested if they could tell me about the subject."

She did not tell them about the worst of the end of Deco-Cake. She would miss him. He wore an initialed handkerchief in his pocket when he came every morning to set up the demonstration booth for her. (How she pretended to struggle with those slats, fight that booth! Here, let me do that, he said.) He tallied the receipts from the day before. He joked, winked, and with a last brow-wrinkling squint at the booth, disappeared into the maze of stores. At evening he came like the evening sun and dismantled the booth. They had discussed lots of things while they were setting up together and dismantling . . . had talked about things Fortune read in the newspaper. She told him she read them every day, she spoke of the bit notices about murders in other lands, unimportant murders, important only to the people murdered. The man had the same breathless immediacy . . . the same magic Robert Preston had in *The Music Man*. His whole style spoke of a wonderful life, a life within one's grasp . . . just around the corner, up that street lined with Ferris wheels and candy-apple concessionaires. That carny charm of his, those stray winks . . . the boss reminded her of a friend of her brother's a long time ago, Hop McElroy. This brother's friend had almost brought her the little orchid corsage . . . and had those been balloons skudding across the gymnasium ceiling? Or had they been testicles . . . airborne? Brightly colored, incandescent, heliumfilled testicles . . . rising, rising, seeking the stratosphere? She had seen the corsage once in a hotel florist's window. The brother's friend had not bought the corsage, however. It was a wrist arrangement of seven speckled sister orchids, small, delicate . . . so translucent and vital, were those petals or was it skin? Human skin that breathed and waited, giving off light? These orchids of her dreams did seem practically human to her. A chorus of little friends. They rode her wrist while she danced the night away. She would take the orchids, siblings, and put them in the icebox. She would look at them every day. But one day, some day, because they were human . . . the brutal air and the harsh eyes of people would turn them brown. But with great grace they would turn that way. And she, Fortune, would know their hour had come. She would remove them from the icebox. And she would make them eternal. Into their original cellophane sack they would go. She pinched shut the bag. She locked it forever with the long, strong florist's pin; the pin had a large pearl-droplet head. Into the old telephone book the shrouded orchids would go. On top went canned foods. She flattened and canonized the wrist corsage of seven friendly orchids.

It seemed as if he, the brother's friend, had brought her the orchids, when all was said and done. She had thought about them so long it almost seemed her one wrist was heavy with them. When she passed florists' windows she compared those bigger, brasher orchids in the window with the ones in her imagination. Years after, she began going to the Elks

Hall dances. She began then to buy herself Saturday night corsages. But she never found the little orchids the brother's friend never brought her. So she could not bear to buy orchids at all. She wore carnations every Saturday night. These were not worth pressing.

Fortune cut her hair off. She went back to reclaim the job. The cake-decorating outfit, she was told, had folded up, moved on. Summer was over; these people go South for Christmas, go to San Diego.

She went to Mammoth. She stood in the lodge next to Biscuit. Fortune was marshaling bobby pins into her new Dynel hairpiece; it was a long, corn-colored fall brighter than doll's hair. The other girls . . . in the lodge, on the slopes . . . whipped their long, true hair into braids and skimmed out onto the snow. Fortune tried the same and tied the end of the Dynel braid with a piece of itself. She stood in front of her ski equipment. Trying hard to look perplexed, so someone would come. A ski instructor in white hair and eyebrows came and buckled her together. She threshed and wallowed around on the beginners' slope. The fall began unbraiding itself. From a distance, however, it must have glinted against her dark parka . . . and the ski instructor saw it . . . he zoomed over and bent over her bindings. She said he came faster than Jack Frost.

That night *aprés*-ski drinking songs began around the fire. *OH THEY HAD TO CARRY HARRY TO THE FERRY OH THEY HAD TO CARRY HARRY TO THE SHORE OH THE REASON THAT THEY HAD TO CARRY HARRY TO THE FERRY WAS THAT HARRY COULDN'T CARRY ANY MORE CALIFORNIA* . . . and here, Bert, the idea is for everyone to outshout for his own state . . .

UTAH or whatever . . . *ARIZONA WASHINGTON NE-*
BRASKA CALIFORNIA I'M HERE TO DO OR DIE AND
HERE'S THE REASON WHY . . . !

She pantomimed and bluffed the lyrics, making robust
notes with a chapped mouth and listing along with the songs.
And, too, she flirted with the ski instructor; Nordic and kind,
he smiled professionally, indulgently, and disappeared onto
the dark snow.

"I don't think that towrope did Miss Grumpet any good,"
Biscuit said.

Campbell said to Fortune, "Have you thought about waitress work, Champ? That's steady."

"Steady," she said. "You said it."

"It might behoove you to listen to somebody with some
experience, Champ."

"Oh? You been a waitress?"

"Look, Champ, we're simply attempting to help you come
down to earth a little bit, come out of orbit."

"You call picking dime tips out of mashed potatoes meeting the public on its own terms?" she said.

❀

Campbell was looking at a repair bill for the Morgan. He
had paid ninety dollars to find out it had been his ski boots
lying on a wire.

Biscuit had sent Fortune and him to the El Rancho. Bal-
ancing a bag of groceries, Fortune told him she had been
hired six hours ago by one of the major firms on the West
Coast.

Campbell stopped, shifted his groceries. "Just what kind
of a job?"

"It is in the physical-fitness field."

"Oh?"

Why was he taking his tie off? He was always taking something off when he talked to a person and rolling it up in a tight snail and setting it on the hood of the car. "Public relations," she said.

"Public relations. I see. In what capacity?"

"Telephone capability."

"I see."

"It is making special offers to people so they will sign up at Gym 'n Trim. That is the name of my company. It is one of the major . . ."

"Interesting you should bring this up, Fortunée. Why, only last night Biscuit and I thought of a job that pays a good wage and you wouldn't have to be sitting all day dialing numbers, soliciting people whose faces you don't even see, Fortunée."

"You do not either see the people's faces you want to buy your pudding either."

"Watch it! That's got nothing to do with it! And don't go around passing judgment on my job! Advertising is something you don't know one goddamn thing about!"

"And, anyway, it does not bother me." She bumped her purse against her thighs. "I do not care if I see my clients' faces. It makes me the *misterioso* behind the voice."

"Would you cut this '*misterioso*' crap! What're you laying on us this *misterioso* crap when we're trying to help you cut the crap!"

Fortune drew away. "Beg pardon? Yes . . . why, yes, Mr. Pudding."

Biscuit's boyfriend slowly pulled off one glove. "Look,

Champ," he said gently, "what Biscuit and I have in mind is just that: saleswork!" He smiled and biffed her on the chin with a flopping glove.

"What do you want me to do? Bite my girlfriend on the lip until the blood comes out like bright paint on the lip?" she said.

"Down at Jiffy Center! Take your pick! Over sixty stores and shops! They need talent down there . . . like you! Somebody down there is looking for somebody with 'that certain subterranean something!' Take Zeigler's, for example."

"Counter work?" She drew away . . . felt the cool hard cans of frozen orange juice pressing into her stomach . . . cold and sensual. "Counter work? What kind of work do you call that? Those girls stand around hitched-up half asleep waiting for some customer to trip over their cash register! How much 'talent,' like you say, has a person got to have to do that?"

"I understand their standards are quite high down there at Jiffy Center."

"Could be."

"Or what about Thirty-one Flavors?"

"Oh yes, now there is a real lulu of a place."

"What's the matter with it?"

"Oh, I am not criticizing. 'Far be it from me.' But do you call standing behind a counter like some wooden Indian or making change or giving somebody something they want when they come in to find it in the first place and sure as not me having to wear one of those tacky uniforms! You really call that the kind of position you can hitch your wagon to a star?"

"If you want to know," Campbell said, "I do. Yes, I do."

She said, "Your star. Not mine, buddy."

Beg *pardon?*

You heard me.

Your st . . . ! Get that down in the records before . . . ! But . . . wait. What, exactly, would you tell the court at this time, were you intending the meaning of behind that proclamation you said to him at that time when you said *Your star. Not mine, buddy?*

I *thought* you would like that, Your Honor.

I did not say I liked it, Miss D. I said what was your opinion behind your meaning.

That I do not like him, the man in question, Miss Besqueth's "constant companion," talking cock of the walk to a person! Our audience knows there comes the day that that person, yes, true, I had to "gird my loins" to say it. And do not ask me any more questions to this: He had come down upon the head of F. Dundy for the last time. And if you go around "putting out bad karma" in the face of F. Dundy too much, the day will come that she will rise up in the face of that opinion and say to you: *Your star. Not mine, buddy!!!*

Whew. But . . . then why—answer the audience at your own convenience—does your throat feel bitter with that taste of adrenaline when you say it?

Look, do you or do you not want to hear the end?

BERT: (Sigh) Yes, yes, all right, all right. (Sigh)

PERSON THAT ROSE UP IN THE FACE OF M. CAMPBELL: Then M. Campbell threw his special driving gloves into the Morgan car and heaved the groceries away from me and walked on past me through the Villa Dionysus breezeway. And so that is how it went. The only thing I am "Post Office"-ed about is that *I* would have liked to do the Pilate thing he did with the gloves.

She lay down on the grass, dug her bottom into it. What restlessness! She would like to murder somebody tonight. Nobody in particular. Just anybody who doubted her. The old Caruthers-Gandemutt face came to visit her. Hello, Miss Dundy? The face arrived now as a blank egg-shaped skull lopped off a department-store mannequin. Wearing a toupee. You no doubt do not recall me, Miss Dundy. It has been some while now . . . person such as yourself! Oh, well, congratulations . . . should have known some lucky man would finally snap you up off the market! Oh now . . . not blah blah pretty little head about me! I will get over you. In time. Those computer maters . . . there will be another chance for me. Even though I am not so a fool to go around thinking they have got another bride such as yourself up their sleeve, please, people! I mean, with the class you have got? Come on. Oh no . . . will be all right . . . man has got to go on. Oh blah blah sweet of you . . . lonely bachelor like myself. And blah blah respect you for . . . guess I better go. He will be home in a minute, I expect, and you will want to be getting primped up for him. I am not good enough to lay a hand on the hem of your little finger anyway. Much less plug you. Yes . . . and same to you, Mrs. Dundy! . . . Bye!

Doors . . . doors, always doors, that was the sound of this place. But where are the men, where are they?

They were there, all around. Yet they all seemed to have one name. A name a person would not forget. Some people always "bitched" that they never forgot a face, it was the

81

name that would not stick. She, as for her, she remembered everyone's name. She never referred to Donna Williams' fiancé, Howard, as Harold. She never mistook a Toby for a Tony or a Tom for a Tim, a Judy for a Janey or a Connie for a Carol. One handshake, firm, pulsing! A look in the eye, eye to eye (and you can check me out in Dale Carnegie on that, Bert), and there you had the name forever! No excuse in forgetting a name when names were so vital. More important, however, was the fun of saying, "Hi there, Lenny!" in the driveway. Several cuts above the blanker "Hi." There was no reason to forget a name, no, not when names belonged to people.

And no, it was not so very impossible to memorize *The Dionysus Dateline,* pictures and names. And the capsule histories, hobbies, and pet peeves of each Dionysid. And then meet one in the flesh. And you say, can say: "And how does a fellow from Bakersfield like the big city, the City of Angels, like they say?" Or, "Say, I have been meaning to take up yoga myself. They say it is the way to pray these days." She knew Lenny liked skin diving, Mark was an accountant, Jim —"his friends call him Jumbo"—had once been student body president at West Phoenix High, Mason had goldfish, and Larry C. was building a dune-buggy from scratch. Lyle was a Democrat, Stacey hated getting up early, Lindner had fought in the Korean War, Bill enjoyed blondes, Carl was born in Bismarck, N. Dak., Fats had run the four-forty at Chico State, Conrad claimed to have invented Drop-Trou, Pete spoke pig Latin, and John L.'s happiest moment was when he found his lost contact lens on the sand at Huntington.

(She never again saw The Kleenex Affair People.) She

saw the dentist, twice. He wore, always, Polaroid sunglasses.
He was, in those mirror, bulging glasses, a man from science
fiction. She lay in wait around corners, behind railings, watching him come and go. And there was a girl named Jeanine,
who had a dog. Fortune found her blurb in the *Dateline*. It
said Jeanine was "into champagne, Arlo Guthrie and sun-
sets and that her dog was mostly German shepherd." But
Biscuit was the one to discover in the *Grapevine:*

> ". . . And rapping of Clandestine Couples, what does this
> reporter hear about J. of D Wing, hi, I'm J.'s dog Woofy,
> look for me in there, too! And all we needed was a dog-
> digging dentist, wot, Jeanine? Seems to us there's a lot
> more than the canine-in-common at DW's neighborhood
> Polident Parlor, wot? You can fool some of the people
> some of the time, but when Cupid twangs his magic
> twanger not even Novocain can make a downer out of
> that old familiar wince in that cardio-type muscle, wot
> say, baby, dear neighbor, Dr. F.? The other day when we
> were in for a tartar trim—we detected a pair of pretty
> heavy star-struck eyes on the other end of that waterpick.
> Hey, Dr.?"

"Well, well, well, there's an upper!" Biscuit was saying.
She was tearing the *Grapevine* in half slowly. "And we wish
him all the happiness in the world, don't we?"
"Beg pardon?"

She saw Jeanine go into the recreation hall. She followed
her in but could not find her.
Dionysids were playing Ping-Pong, checkers, passing
around an occasional marijuana joint, grading test papers.
Donna Williams taught sixth grade, and she was there.
"Listen to this," Donna was saying. " 'Sir Francis Drake in-

vented the steamboat!' " There were men sitting backward in chairs, wearing Bermuda shorts and Biblical sandals. These men swung legs muscled like fists over the chairs; they straddled the chairs, like Marlon Brando. Donna, the teacher, made red gashes across the test papers of sixth-grade children. The crotches of the men straddling the chairs bulged rudely. The bulges seemed to be protesting: Freedom! I am trapped in here like something limp and puzzling. I am like the dead bait, mollusks, maybe, on the damp, slimy docks by the ocean.

The jukebox played José Feliciano, ". . . *because I want to . . . porque yo quiero. . . .*" Fortune made Latin-beat clicking sounds with her tongue and she moved her shoulders in a dancy, south-of-the-border way. "Hi, gang!" she said.

"Hello, Chiquita Banana," said a man eating sunflower seeds. He spit the hulls in his hand. "Sit down."

She asked him later if he was a doctor by any chance.

"Me?"

"Yes," said Fortune.

"No. What makes you ask that?"

It was his hands, she told him; any day of the week she could pick out a man of medicine. "But I guess I went wrong this time."

The man said, "But, I mean, what would make you think my hands are a doctor's?" He was friendly. He smiled at her. She did not know his name. "What is it about them?" He stared at her. "That's too much you should say that. I wanted to be a doctor when I was a kid."

"What are you waiting for??? Go get 'em! The sky is the oyster!"

"You're a nice girl," he said. "What's your name? Those are a real pair of mink earrings, I'll bet." He touched her ear, fondled it. "Yeah, that's real mink, all right."

She spoke through a supersonic buzzing in her head, faint, constricted. Then he was touching the right lobe—was that his hand?—and said she must be connected with a hospital or something, the way she knew things.

"Pudding Tain brings you New Dessert Discovery! Empire Flavors! When at home eat as the Romans would! Colossus Caramel! . . . SPQR Strawberry! . . . Chariot Chocolate! . . . Roman Raspberry! . . . (then *segue* to . . .) *Render unto your palate that which Caesar would!* (and *super* of . . .) *Pudding Tain—The Imperial Dessert.* How's that sound, B?"

Fortune untangled the telephone cord from around the stool's leg. She stepped over Campbell, reading his advertising copy on the floor.

Biscuit was also on the floor, cutting, sewing, making pillow covers and drapes and things for Campbell's apartment; they were redecorating it entirely in black and white. Most of the labor took place in B-12, since Milo's place was being repainted and carpeted. "Oh, sweetie, that's really the heaviest thing you've done! 'Empire Flavors!' How you ever think of those things. You genius!"

Fortune dialed and was singing: *"Tweeeeeeeeedlee tweedlee tweedlee dee! I am as happy as can be! Jimminy crickets, jimminy jax! You make my heart go clickety-clack! Tweedlee tweedlee dee!"* She had played nervous, ferocious, committed Ping-Pong with the man in the "rectum" hall, as he had called it. The man—he never told his name, she never asked it—had smacked his paddle through the air in long, ghostly strokes. The ball chased her, escaped her, flirted with her! That little white Ping-Pong ball had seemed to have its own kinetic *duende*. It came to her all as the sing-along dot in the old movie shorts, follow-the-bouncing-ball. And the moon would always fly down out of the sky to become the bouncing ball.

"Yes, and we are going to send you free, Mrs. Holloway, yes, free! Without any charge to you, no, none, Gym 'n Trim is going to send you our special offer! Beg pardon? Our special diploma, free and good for the first two sessions of our courses at our salon! Now, tell us when we can put you down for an appointment to solve you or your husband's particular figure. . . ."

"No problem," the woman said.

"Well, and are you not the lucky citizens! Well, then, say, why not come on down and just get a muscle tone then? That is all you 'perfect figure' types need . . . and now, I know what you are going to say and I will eat my hat if there is any obligation. . . ."

The woman hung up. Fortune said, "Some of these old sows do not want to come around at all."

But Biscuit was sanding a chair from the Salvation Army. All the furniture for Campbell's redecoration was to be black. He squatted next to her, sanding. Biscuit's buttocks rolled with the rhythm of her efforts. Fortune watched her shearing the epidermis off the chair, those haunches rolling, rolling like a galleon bearing into the wind, grunting.

". . . California's foremost figure control and body center. And I bet you did not know we have got a couple of stars

86

from the Fox lot that use us. I do not recall their names but take my word for it. We have got the cream de la cream, Miss Iz, and hold onto your hat now! It is F . . . R . . . E . . . E, that is right, Free . . . !"

She went to the refrigerator and pulled out the vegetable bin. Two oranges furry with mildew rolled down to meet her. She found a box of Quaker Puffed Rice and ate those dry from the box. She lay with the box on her chest, dribbling the cereal "shot from guns" into her mouth. She thought of films on birth; dripping, purple, the newborn was laid on the mother's chest like the box here. The baby's tubes and nodules gleamed with membranes.

Biscuit and Campbell left; she heard the door close. The telephone directory flooshed onto the floor. She lay and thought of the stars and the comets and the machine at the bottom of the sea, that keeps grinding out salt.

Later she got hold of somebody in the R's in East L.A., who said he thought she sounded awfully cute over the telephone.

He promised to buy anything from Gym 'n Trim if only he could meet that voice behind it all. "Sure like the sound of your little voice," he said.

His name was Rusty.

I liked the sound of his voice, too, Bert.

But she was certainly not going to say so. (Rule Number Nix: Do Not Let the Man Blah Blah Blah You Are Interested Too Early. "Keep Him Guessing.")

❋

A song was in order then. All the next day it stayed in her head. It was Sergio Mendez. It was "The Look of Love."

What came out was the tag end. A long, love-soaked fila-ment, ". . . *can't deny-yyyyyyyy!*" She and Rusty talked on the telephone again the following night. Rusty told her to "listen to me on the radio, babe."

8

A Dionysid named Gary Walker was driving to MacArthur Park, was going there in an old surfing woody crammed with people in sweatshirts, workshirts, T-shirts. In the back with the bats and gloves was Donna Williams and her visiting "betrothed," a person of the Hebrew religion. Howard scooted over, making room for Fortune. Donna was singing, ". . . *buy me some peanuts and Cracker Jacks, I don't care if I never . . . !*"

Howard smiled at Fortune. ". . . *if they don't win it is a shame!*" Fortune sang.

"Gymnasium? I thought you were working for that cake-decorating thing?" Donna said.

". . . *so it is one! two! three! and you are out . . .* Correction there, Donna: figure-control firm. And, no, I left Deco-Cake behind 'in my dust' some while back . . . *at the old ball ga-aaaaaaaaaaaaaaaaaaaaame!*"

Bliss welled in her. Life was coming to a head this afternoon. Nothing else was necessary but the here, the now! This ship cutting through this sunshine! Skipper Gary, hands on the wheel, big tumor of a ring on his middle finger, ΣAE OHIO STATE UNIVERSITY '59, leading the songs! Yes, the only place! Here! The only motto: Hang in There, like they said.

Saturday afternoon and everybody's "hang-ups" had been "hung up," Bert. Hung up with the lunch pail or briefcase or whatever at the end of a work-a-Dionysid week . . . freeways . . . pharmacy counter lunches, rut, stress, maybe boredom and pangs of unrequited love, who knew? Out the window! All these now blew away, trailed away, became the wake of the going, gunning *Good Ship Woody* packed with wild-eyed—here we are!—good people over twenty-five but under forty. We sing together! Wow, Bert, we are *heavy!* *"Salvation Army! Salvation Army! Put a nickel in the drum, save another drunken bum!"*

"Testimony!!"

"All the women shall wear . . . suits of armor!"

"BOOOOOOOOOOOOOOOO!"

". . . But all the men shall carry can openers!"

"HOOOOOOOOOOOOOOOORAY!"

See what I mean, Bert? Ragged but right! Hang-ups? Boo! Down with them! Down with Reagan, Nixon, Agnew, hemorrhoids, yellow teeth, bad English, war, peace, blackheads, pimples, and trusses! Up with us! Yaaaaaaaaay! Up with let it all hang out! No keeping DWers down! We are going to tear the guts clean out of Saturday! Raaaaaaaay! Down with the Over Forty! Hooray! Down with you next door in your Cadillac and cigar and your wife—your wife there with pearl chains hooked to her reading glasses so she can find them without too much trouble, so her own glasses, her own possessions do not run away from her! Up yours, Mr. Cigar and Mrs. Glasses! We will run you and your twenty-five air-conditioned anniversaries right off this boulevard! Raaaay for us! Raaay for the Certain Subterraneans. "I left that Deco-Cake position a while back, I said! I LEFT

THAT DECO-CAKE . . . ME, THAT CAKE PEOPLE WHILE BACK!" Salvation Arm-mee! Salvation AAAAR-RRRmy! Put a nickel in the DRUM! Save another drunken BUM! Testimony! All the women shall wear grass skirts! Boooooo! But all the men—ah-*hah!*—shall drive LAWN-MOWERS!!! What? HOOOOOOOOORAAaaay! Salvation AAAAARM-my!

The Band-Aid taped over the nail inside her shoe was loosening. She dropped back behind the other Dionysids to retape it. Standing on one foot, she held onto a drinking fountain. She could hear the men. The smacking mantle of their red-bloodedness hung over the softball diamond. "Sock it to me, you mothers!" "Yaaaaaaah . . . yer ass!" The men, whipping up the air, razzing, jeering, hawking. This sound, males at their malest, came to her as love and Oz incarnate. It seemed the great and sudden I AM awaiting her behind the veil of bushes and Cyclone fencing.

Bare-chested, there was Campbell, the top half of his body . . . the bats, the gloves. And Ollie, the big "spade," Bert. Ollie was bare-chested, too, standing in the sun, his back as slick as an eggplant. Campbell sauntered up to bat and knocked a humiliating grounder down the line to third base. Then there came Renz, who worked at Lockheed, and Renz lobbed the ball to first base slowly, no sweat, people, that ball will arrive. Then someone came home. This runner heaved himself against the backstop amid a cloud of cheers and jeers and whistles.

Fortune watched all this from under the bleachers.

She was crouching there, hiding.

She had been running to catch up with the others, after

91

taping her shoe, when the sun glanced off a pair of Polaroid sunglasses.

There across the field—a mile! a millennium! on the horizon, like lightning or the Song of Solomon—came the dentist.

He was wearing an alpaca sweater, mustard-colored.

He was bouncing a set of car keys in the air.

That moment, that millennium, was when she, Fortune, had done the thing that she . . .

. . . do not at this time care to explain, Bert.

She had run under the bleachers to hide. The staggered planks, the shadows, the legs aided her, abetted her. She was terrified to move. *Take me out to the ball game!!!* Her legs doubled under her began to throb . . . *Cracker Jacks! I do not care if I ever get back! Oh root root-root for the home team . . . if they do not win it is a shame!*

She duck-walked slowly—God in his heaven above would only know how slowly—cautiously, she moved through the candy wrappers and rumpled cigarette packages. The spike heels on her shoes made this difficult. She spread out a newspaper, a shoppers' news . . . only the barest of cracklings. She sat down on it. She unbent her legs and rubbed them, picking off a Sno-cone cup impaled on the end of a spike heel. Less than a foot from her head was a row of feet. These sprouted into calves. Voices from above identified the feet: Marguerite Parker, Janet Manfire, Lynn Peterson, Marilyn Stanwood Reid, Grisdale LaFleur's girlfriend . . . other people. . . . Some tapped ashes; like artificial snow they filtered down through the sunlit cracks of the bleachers. Slits, spaces, peek-holes appeared in the shadows. She could see Gary Walker through them. Next to him, Weldon Cerkvenik and Grisdale LaFleur. Gris was cracking his knuckles. Now came

Milo Campbell, jiggling back and forth, socking his fist into his softball glove. Above his sweat pants an elastic band could be seen from . . .

. . . the real name is "athletic supporter," Bert.

And where was . . . ? Ah, he could not be seen, no; the mystic dentist had drifted into the wings, fading, fading. . . .

Somebody burly, a bear of a man, stepped up to the plate and slammed the bat against the bare air. Then he swung and missed the ball twice.

Campbell cackled, "Hey, Casey! Can't mix it up today, stud, or what? Mudville, yay-y!"

The burly man tapped the plate and danced and told the pitcher to put it right there, you mother humper, let them see if the pitcher could pitch. Now Biscuit moved into view of the shadowed peek-hole. She had been uncasing beer. Now she disappeared. Fortune then sensed the bleachers quivering. She moved slowly, quietly through the debris under the bleachers until she was sitting under . . .

. . . him.

She could read his shoes. Cat's Paw . . . God, how human he was! How fragile he was! A repaired rubber heel on his shoe! His socks went up, up . . . too far . . . there was no flesh to be seen. The dentist, his own man, turned his wasp's head in his Flash Gordon glasses . . . and his glance disintegrated the bleachers beneath him.

Fortune froze.

"And what'samatta with the dentist, hey, big boy?" This was Campbell's voice. Now she could see Campbell. He was pinching his nostrils. He hitched officiously at the strap of his "jockstrap." What was *he* trying to prove? Yes, Mr. Boyfriend, we know you are trying to remind yourself you are still there! "What'samatta with the dentist? Something un-American about softball? Hey?"

"Honey!" Biscuit called to Campbell. "Didn't you hear me? I said your jockstrap is showing! Do you want some beer?" Biscuit, too, was overhead. She sat now, wrestling with the beer cans. "Your little girlfriend isn't here," she said. Now she was talking to the dentist.

"Something un-American about softball?" This was Campbell again, calling from behind the Cyclone backstop.

The dentist said: "I'm not a member. So I can't play." How level! What a voice! It seeps down into the bleachers, down through the sun slats and shadows. It barely rattles the Three Musketeers wrapper.

How Fortune remembered the sound of it . . . after all these months. He had said the Fourth of July: "I'm not a member. I'm just using your grass for a shortcut, okay?" And then he had said—or had not said, who knew?—"I will meet you back here when the party is over." Or maybe he had said: "They tell me you have never been pl***** before. Word has got it that you are still in your natural state. We will take care of that. If you ever have any trouble—with your *teeth*, that is—why do you not come up and see me sometime?" Although Bert insisted that the dentist had said: "Why do you not pick me up and smoke me sometime?" But she had argued back, through the months, that the dentist had said: "I will meet you back here when the party is over."

Biscuit was saying to him, "I always thought you hated dogs." She sat down next to him on the bleachers.

The dentist laughed.

"I always wanted a puppy," Biscuit said. "A little baby furry puppy . . . and you said no. I always thought you hated dogs. And now, there it is, for everybody to read, you're screwing some girl in the club who owns a German shepherd."

"Who told you that?" he said.

"Or maybe you're screwing her dog and not her."

"Yeah, maybe so," said Skip Fritchey, and he rises and leaves because Jeanine has arrived, and they walk together across the baseball field and out of the park.

9

The burly man struck out, a bad sport. Furious, he hurled the bat. It struck Campbell in the head. He had been hanging on the backstop, hitching at his athletic supporter, shouting at the dentist when this with the bat happened.

Now he lay on the bed in B-12, a cold washcloth molded to his head. Biscuit whisked around, telling Fortune to prepare some hot bouillon for him.

"No!" said Campbell. "Don't go pouring that shit down my throat. Just go and get dressed. Just go on and go to the goddamned party without me."

"Without you, Daddy?"

"Yes, goddamn it. You only want to see Fritchey anyway."

"Don't be silly, honeypot. Besides, if he goes, he'll be there on Jeanine's guest coupon . . . the one with that dumb dog and would you believe boobs hanging to her knees. Besides, he won't be there. He hates parties. Oh, don't think I don't know a thing or two about the bastard. He hates parties. Oh, Daddy, how adorable! You look so cute when you're jealous—or is it because of that dear, dear rag on your head? And, Daddy, doll, don't use vulgar words about the bouillon."

"Yeah, yeah, go on to the party. Take the Morg, go on,

that's what you're waiting for. And be sure to strip the gears while you're at it."

*

Biscuit went and got dressed, hogging the bathroom. "You're delirious, darling," she kept saying to Campbell over her shoulder. "Lie back. Roomie, get him a napkin. I'm going to get some of that bouillon down him."

"You're still hot for his ass. . . ."

"Milo, I forbid you to use that word! Here, drink up!"

He lifted his head, drank like an old man. "Watch second gear. I'm going to send the Champ here along with you to see that that cunt-hunter doesn't come sniffing around."

"Daddy!"

"You with me on that, Champ?"

"Beg pardon?" Fortune had been trying to slip her underwear out of a dresser drawer unnoticed.

"I said I want you to keep an eye on Fritchey tonight at Trader Vic's to see he keeps his gearshift in neutral where Biscuit's concerned. Her and him I can't trust. You I can trust."

"I am sorry," said Fortune. "I will not be going to the cocktail party."

"What? Really? Why not, Roomie? You could ride over with me. Not going? What's the matter?"

"I have got a date this evening, if you care to know my business, and I can see you are bound, you are determined."

"A *date?*" Biscuit set the cup of bouillon down. "Well, would you believe! Isn't that terrifo, Rooms, terrifo! Who with, Roomie?"

"Nobody you people know," she said.

"Hey, hey, hey. There's a glint in your eyes, Roomie! Now don't go springing a wedding on us next weekend!"

"I will not be springing a wedding on you, Beverly."

"Yeah, well, with you, you never know. You and your flitting and ostrich feathers and cloak and dagger . . . and the weirdo other life you probably lead when you're not around here. Well, I'm off, kids. Milo, you sleep. Do not move from that bed until I get back. Roomie, before he crashes, you get the rest of that bouillon down him. Thanks. I don't know what I'd do without you, Fortunée. You know that, don't you? *Ciao*."

Campbell turned over. He readjusted the washcloth on his forehead. "Wet this again, will you?" He tossed the washcloth onto the night table.

"I have got to get ready for my date," Fortune said. "Can you be as kind as to go in to the couch?"

"Move? With this head?"

"All right. I will take my things, every last little bobby pin and everything, into the bathroom and be inconvenient in there, then!"

"Right on. But wet this cloth first, will you?"

She picked up the cloth by one scrofulous corner and carried it into the kitchen.

"You pick up on that number she was laying on me? That big hurry she was in?" Campbell called. "Just couldn't wait to get to the party, could she? Shee-yit."

"Beg pardon?"

"She doesn't give a rat's ass that I'm like this. I could have a f***ing concussion, you know."

"Yes, you do it enough with her to give you a concussion, that is for sure."

"You wetting that rag?" he said.

"She said for me to feed you the rest of this soup."

"Let her douche with it."

"Here's your washcloth," said Fortune.

"You put it on, will you? You know, the way she did it. Kind of pat it down."

She lay the cloth on his forehead, molding it the way Biscuit had done.

Campbell said, "Who's your date with?"

"A person."

"Jesus, I know! I mean, who is he?"

"Someone I met on my own. Not through this club and its promises, its deals."

"You're always cutting out on your own. What do you do? Where do you go?" He turned over on his side, wincing and pressing the washcloth to his forehead.

"Places."

"Look, Champ, you don't have to play clandestine rip-off with me! I don't give a shit where you go or what you do."

"Well, the other day I went to the LaBrea Tar Pits, for one thing. And the movies, of course. But with my job, I have not got time for philandering around anymore."

"Get me some ice, will you? In a towel. I need cold right on my frontal lobes."

"I will do it if you will then go in to the couch," she said.

He agreed. She brought the ice, and he said, "So you're not going to tell us who your date's with. Wait a minute . . . you going out with Fritchey?"

"No!!! Why ever would you say that? No, I am not!"

"I don't know. Biscuit said you really had the hots for him. I just thought maybe."

" '*The* . . . !' Mister, I have not got the . . . 'hots' for anybody if you are interested in my opinion on the situation! And as for her, she has not got to go around telling people she can outguess what is her opinion is in my head! *And as for me, I have not got that word for a single living human being on this earth!!!*"

"Okay, okay. Hey, come on back here with that ice," he said.

"*Here is your fool ice!!!*"

"You do it, please. You put it on my head."

"You said you would go on the couch!"

"I will if you put the ice on my head. Kind of rub it around on the soreness."

She did, but then he said he changed his mind and was going back on his end of the bargain. "I'll tell you what," he said. "I'll go in there and let you get dressed in peace if you give me a little kiss."

"Beg pardon?"

"Come on. A little wet one. It'll fix my head up."

Again she said beg pardon.

"Jesus Christ! How many times do I have to say it? Kiss me!"

"*Kiss* you?"

"She wrinkles up her face, oh, Christ-o. Come on, Champ. I have this head on me like a jackhammer. I need a little nursing. Give me a kiss. Come on, I won't look. Then I'll go in to the couch. Better than that—I'll split to my own bed."

"But I do not want to kiss you!"

"The hell you don't," Campbell said.

"That is right—the hell!"

"When was the last time you were laid, Champ?"

"Yes, and I am happier a thousandfold times by far than some people I know that that is not their problem to complain about and that *lie* when they say they will take ice and go to the couch and do not and lie, lie, lie!!!"

"I ought to f*** you right now and get your mind right. You know, you're not a very together chick. Did you know that? You just can't seem to get it together, can you? Still, there's nothing wrong with you that a good balling wouldn't set straight. You wouldn't be so goddamned up-tight all the time if you made it with somebody more often. When was the last time? With that cracker Deco-Cake manager? Come on over here, Champ, and quit playing the late, late movie with me, Bette Davis. Hey, come on over here . . . and, yeah, say, this ice couldn't hurt. You'll thank me for this."

10

Rusty should mean red hair. It should mean pale eyebrows, pinkish and strange and benign. The name also should mean freckles splattered on the arms and a riot of freckles huddling together on the cheeks, backs of hands, and she was prepared even from the first moment she heard Rusty's name on the telephone to forgive red hair and peach coloring and large freckles searching for one another.

Rusty drove a Buick. That was one of the things he had told her over the telephone: "Me and my Buick. . . ."

So Fortune, in her head, began to hear rhythm 'n blues, oldies, goodies, a song that came back: *"How would you like to go ridin' in my Buick fifty-nine . . ."* A song from her adolescence . . . only it was way back, had nothing to do with the year 1959; it was 1956, maybe, with that song. *"Uh-don't be mad at me, boys, if your bucket don't ride like mine. Buick fifty-nine, Buick FIFty-nine. . . ."*

Rusty came out of the dark, spinning in the dark gravel of the Villa in a Buick convertible, his radio blaring, his hair black in the yellow lights of the driveway, his radio squalling with platter chatter, baby, coming at you now!

Who would know, ever know in this universe, what the name Rusty did or did not mean over the telephone? Red hair, black hair! Names "schmames"! Names were not all they were "cracked up to be."

Rusty's hair could have been red. But it was dyed blacker than bootwax.

At that time, Miss Dundy, during the ongoing of the evening were you able to notify yourself that you were an "F"? . . . that stands for fool.

A telephone. Bland, black, deceitful. A person would do best in the future not to look to it to guide her toward the dimly flickering lights of truth.

". . . Fortune—yes, rhymes with flowers-in-May—Dundy, with a special offer for you from Gym 'n Trim! I did get you out of bed, Mr. Russell?" Those were her first words with Rusty.

Rusty had chuckled, liquid, slow. . . . "Yes, you did, you Fortunée Dundy, you."

They had talked on the telephone twice . . . long trial-balloon conversations . . . probing . . . toying. She had then begun to tell Rusty the things in her head. And Rusty was a listener, one of the world's few listeners in this life of ours. Rusty, with that voice like molasses. "Listen to me on the radio, babe."

Over the radio, Rusty's voice had been all the more arousing. He had told her to tune in to station WRAP, ". . . in the wee, wee morning hours, babe, you be up, hear!" Ring, ring, bleep, bleep, Bert, one of those shows, a talk program. Greater L.A. called in, aired itself to "Maurice the Ear." Vietnam, dirty air, water and streets, dying fish and oil-covered ducks, methedrine and methadone, and to invite the public to drag races organized under the National Hot Rod Association. People called to complain about private

things, but mostly about public things. Rusty told Fortune
to listen between three and four A.M. Friday morning. She
should be alert for a question about when was Maurice the
Ear going to get on the bandwagon backing the Sappho
Society.

"Rusty?" Maurice said. *"You again?"*

*"Yeah, Maury, I've got a little matter here I'd like to take
up about Butches for Peace. . . ."*

*"Look, Rusty, God love your heart, I'd love to, but I've
got a lady on the other line out in Venice that's got something on her mind about the citrus pickers' strike. Catch
you later."*

"Hold on a minute, Maury. . . ."

(How important Rusty's voice sounded over the radio!
How distant . . . it filtered and crackled . . . invincible
and electronic.)

". . . this'll just take a minute, Maury," Rusty said.

"Catch you some other time . . . bleep *. . . Hello, Venice? M the E here, your talk-a-thon king, the ice-cool catalyst
fielding your feelings midnight to morning. Spread it on me,
Ven."*

The first thing she said to Rusty upon climbing into the
car—after how do you do—was: "I heard you on the radio."
Rusty, spinning that Buick convertible out of the drive as
if it were a flaming chariot—runaway horses! to our death,
you and me, babe!—said Maurice the Ear was a hawk, they
should not let a dangerous man like that on the radio.

Then they were out on the freeway. They cut through the
air with the top down; Fortune's fall whipped about like
frayed rope, and the ends of it bit into her face when she

turned her head away. She was trying not to study Rusty. Do Not Act Too Surprised on a Blind Date. Keep Him Guessing Why He Does Not Surprise You.

Rusty took her to a bar on Sunset Strip, called The Toklas, and they sat in a booth with Rusty's friends. Rusty held her hand and showed her pictures of people strapping on plastic phalluses. Some of the friends had just returned from Copenhagen—from the Sexpo '70—and they later passed around other pictures of people with Pepsi-Cola bottles held between their legs. "We call ourselves the Pepsi Generation," said one of Rusty's friends. And everybody laughed at "Frank," who was a woman, but who was, indeed, "frank." They were the frankest table, the ribaldest booth in the bar. "Rusty" was not Ora Russell's real Christian name, it turned out. No, "Rusty" was the nickname. Her friends called her that. And even the bar had changed its name. Before World War II it had been named the Aloha.

She knew what to do in an emergency. You go to the Yellow Pages.

11

So do not think, Bert, you can fool F. Dundy.

Under *T* for Taxi, and she told the cab driver about it.
"F. Dundy will not be fooled twice," she said also.

She said the same thing to Biscuit, that F. Dundy would
not be fooled twice.

Biscuit said, "Uh-unh, once is enough. Uh-unh, no go,
talking to every pervert in L.A. over *my* telephone? Oh-ho-
no, sweetie pie, not in this house!"

"You can understand, Champ," Campbell said, "that Biscuit wouldn't want just anyone to have this telephone listing,
can't you? And, well, I don't want these strange types to
have her number, either. You don't need to talk to these
strange people over the telephone, do you, Champ?"

"That is according to your opinion about that word
'strange.' 'Strange' could be all around us. 'Strange' could be
right here in this very club or even right here in this same
apartment, with biting down on lips and bringing blood, if
you care to ask my opinion on the subject of the word
'strange.' "

"We just don't see the necessity for this." Now Campbell
was stroking Biscuit's hair. She sat at his feet. They looked

106

like a dowager and her dog on a pillow . . . stroking, their voices stroke, Campbell's voice, in long strokes, travels from his mouth, sifts through his moustache, his new goatee. "You understand our position, I'm sure."

"Roomie, darling, listen to what Milo is trying to say. We love you. And, naturally, we're concerned about you, that's all. You have lots of nice men friends here in the club to talk to. You don't need to get hung up with this other sort of thing—these sickies, these bull dikes—and on the telephone, on top of it all. Gee, Rooms, there are *other* people, you know?"

"You name me one," Fortune said.

"You have the guys in Dionysus West, Roomie! Look around you!"

"Yes, and where are they then? Where they are! That is what I would be interested to have somebody tell me on the situation! Where are all these men supposed to be wining a person, dining a person if she joins this club? Yes, the boy-friends of people do say to a person they will 'get her mind right' and use ice and do things because she is crying because she really needs that kind of favor that is a favor only in *his* mind's eye not mine! And the other is that I paid my money, and where are the men? I do not yet see the other end of the bargain!"

"Be patient, Roomie."

"Be patient, Champ."

She carried some Gym 'n Trim certificates into the bedroom. She returned and stood in the kitchenette eating some Quaker Puffed Rice from the box. She carried it with her out onto the balcony. She said to Biscuit, "You going to take the telephone away from me?"

107

12

The Ora Russell Affair obsessed her. She was sure that she was turning into a lesbian, she, Fortune. Her desire was regurgitating all over itself . . . retreating, curling back, doubling back upon its own kind! Looking to its own kind for a complement! *Oh, where? Where to?* She wept. Later she was sure she was turning into a man, against her wishes. She, Fortune, her female organs, dwindling, so long abeyant, were now slowly changing. Her glands and hormones were in riot. She watched for whiskers on her upper lip. Her organs were turning . . . her breasts, were they flatter, even flatter? She examined herself . . . Down There. She read. She looked in encyclopedias in the Los Angeles Public Library. Somewhere, some sentence, some idiot genius doctor or writer said that a woman's tiny ridge Down There was a cheap, pathetic, shriveled imitation, hopeful, hopeless, a pining, tiny version of a man's long strong You Know What. The thought that she was halfway to becoming a man . . . ! She forgot she was a virgin. She was obsessed now that she was a hermaphrodite. She always had known she was, anyway. When the other girls in gym class had their periods at twelve and thirteen, she did not have hers until fifteen. She should have known then the message! That secret! Those menses trying to tell her something! Why did she not listen to them?

Miss Dundy, what good would listening have done? Would you tell the court what you would have done different in your lifetime, beg pardon?

She was sick, sickened by these new facts.

*

"You're a guh-guh-guhroovy good group, katz and jammers!" This was television's Randy, the emcee on PAIR-OFF! ". . . look-see to find out who's our first PAIR-OFF! pair today! Who's it gonna be this week, katz and jammers, who's it GONNA BE???"

The screen split vertically. A nymph appeared on the left, flicking back sheets of tinsely hair. Keen of eye and nostril, she bit her lip for the camera. She sat on a throne; the back was shaped in a giant valentine. (If only there were no throne! Fortune fussed with the "contrast" dial.)

Three heart-shaped holes in a backdrop flashed onto the screen, to the right. Grin by grin, three young men popped their faces in these holes. The drums rolled. The emcee shouted: "All-lall-lall right, Mystery Girl! Let's us let you grab a listen up to your unseen Mystery Men Numbers ONE . . . TWO . . . THREE!"

Mystery Man Number One said—and his voice, strained basso, plowed through the orchestra's cymbals—"Hel-lo, Mystery Girl." Numbers Two and Three said: "Howdy there, Mystery Gal" and "Bonjour, Mademoiselle Mystery."

The Mystery Girl continued fooling with her lip. She lay forefinger to cheek—which to choose, which to choose? She gripped the arms of the throne. She bowed her lovely head, listening, and her hair dripped down about her body, a silver cataract . . . descending.

She deserves that throne, Bert.

"All right, katz and jammers, all right now!!!" The emcee was beside himself. *"Mystery Girl, now that you've had a chance to listen to the hellos of our hand-picked heroes, let's us find out if these young whippersnappers think as good as they sound!"*

The Mystery Girl freed her face of the shimmering hair. She read a card in her hand. *"Mystery Man Number One . . . if you were stranded on a desert island with me . . ."* And later, *"Who was Thomas Edison? (A) in the field of entertainment? (B) in the field of . . ."* And *"Number Three, sell me a dimple!"*

And so on until someone won. Pan American flew the first PAIR-OFF! couple to Honolulu . . . with prizes of portable hair dryers and hot combs and passes to Marineland. The same went to two other Mystery Girls and Men; trips were to the Bahamas and Acapulco, where Randy promised the third couple they would have "mucho fun-o."

❁

To Who It Might Concern Hello I am a new person in town and I was wondering what are the chances of being a Mystery Girl there happen to be a lot of things about me that have got that certain air about it to other people that mystery air if we have got to call it that. And I will say at this time that it is true there is a lot about me that is mysterious to them. You have got yourselves quite a little television show there if you get what I mean one time I was at a state fair and a man looking for girls for a pageant said I think you have got style how would you

110

like to travel around the country and maybe later be in a movie or on television since we got the idea looking at you dancing there at the pavilion that you have got that certain something that makes people sit up and take notice of a person such as yourself the pageant needs you you dance good and could travel around this country meeting people and dancing with the men and boys anybody that has got a pair of eyes in his head can see you have got what men call class the way they were lined up to dance with you at the dance pavilion the other side of the Home Show Building what do you say there is something about the way you dress the way you talk the way you dance we cannot say as we can call it a name or it has not got one it is just that something mystery about you and then there was the time I was riding the bus minding to my own things when what happens I notice a mirror over the bus driver's head and his eyes are on that mirror until I had to turn my eyes off the mirror because he was looking so hard same problem I have got something deep and unknown inside me that makes them want to say hold on a minute miss I got ahold of your eyes in the mirror and I am not the same since same problem with men and mirrors and I know how to meet the public on its own terms and I would just like to say to you at this time that you have got yourself quite a program there PAIR-OFF! the way you bring a girl and a man together you send them to Hawaii now there is an idea I admire it is a state where people are dreaming to go not only that but not too long ago a while back I had a success as one of the topnotch pastry designers on the West Coast my firm was planning to send me to open a branch in Phoenix or New York but I said thank you but no thank you gentlemen I take your offer as an honor I will stay right here in this state if you do not mind here is where my life is shaping up Oh come on Miss Dundy then how about at least making one little business trip to show

our product but then I had an offer and success from one
of the largest figure control firms on the West Coast so
when you are picking girls for PAIR-OFF! keep in mind
Fortunée Dundy we will be a blue ribbon team I have got
respect for a show such as yourself that makes so many
young couples find each other also I have been selected
for the famous club Dionysus West and that is another
thing to keep in mind when you are thinking of

F. Dundy

She attached these several sheets of mauve stationery to
the application blank and sent along the snapshot of herself
with the Fourth of July trophy.

PAIR-OFF! answered the following week. She was not
eligible. She had not read the entry blank very well; she
was six years over the age limit. But she was invited to be
a guest of the show and participate in the studio audience.
She tacked up a notice on the Bacchus Bulletin Board.

> TO Who It Might Concern Dionysid F. Dundy
> is going to be on the television show PAIR-OFF!
> if you want to "get it all together" and team up
> and get behind a member watch her she will be
> the one in the black dress with the chantilly
> sleeves.

"I will be the one in the black dress," she told Biscuit and
Campbell. "Do you ever notice how Randy, the emcee, always picks someone to interview at half-time that is sitting
next to the aisle? People always do things the easiest way,
and he is no different. I will be in black chantilly. I will be
next to the aisle. You two watch for me. Afterward, you tell
me how I sounded. Will you?"

But the program was video-taped. So the following week Biscuit made a party for Fortune, inviting another couple for dinner, from E Wing. The man was an old surfer, his skin like mica. "Hobie," said his T-shirt. The woman, Cheryl —what a voice, Bert, scratch your fingernails over a blackboard—helped Biscuit break out the TV tables. Through the clattering of silverware, Campbell lay on the couch clipping his nails with a key-ring nail clipper.

The old surfer is acting like it is his house, Bert, the way he takes over the channel selector.

Fortune switched the channel back to PAIR-OFF!

". . . *measure up in the intellect department!*" Randy was shouting.

"*Okay, Mystery Man Number Three,*" said the Mystery Girl. "*Was the play* Hamlet *written by* (A) *Jacqueline Susann,* (B) *George Plimpton,* (C) *William Shakespeare?*"

"Daddy, put napkins. Roomie, hand these to Milo."

Randy groaned. ". . . *Sorry we are! You men have to watch these questions! They're trickier than the devil from time to time! . . .*"

The man in the Hobie T-shirt jabbed his arm into the air and twiddled his fingers at Cheryl: "Salt."

Fortune said, "In real life that Mystery Girl has got split ends on that hair of hers. It does not look it on television. Television makes everything look different."

"*Okay, Mystery Man Number One: Tell me,*" said the girl, "*what good is a girl if she doesn't know how to kiss?*"

❋

"*Okay, then, katz and jammers! Hah hah hah hah! She chose him because he had 'a cute hello'! Okay, let's us give a look-see at just what is behind that cute hello! Will Number Two step out from behind our . . ."*

Then, finally, chuckling and snapping the microphone cord behind him, the emcee was moving up the aisle. He asked who he had here today.

"Roomie, it's you!"

"SHHHHHHHHHHH! Is that me? Yes, that is me! Is that really what I look like? No! Really? Do I look like that?"

"You look great! Doesn't she?"

"*. . . and so how are you liking California?*" the emcee was saying to her televised self.

This self was looking away from the microphone. It was searching for the camera it presumed was in search of her. "*To level with you, Randy, you have got yourself quite a little state here! Did you know that?*"

"*Well, we like it. And we're sure glad you do, Mrs. Dundy.*"

"*No, I am not some lucky man's 'better half' quite yet, Randy! Bachelor gal 'from the word go.' But we hope not for long! Ho ho ho. And I will just put in one more word here to all those fellows out there in Bachelorland: Hi, guys. If you happen to be in the market for a maiden . . .*"

"*You betcha . . . !*" Randy was saying. He tried to withdraw the microphone. "*Well, thank you for being with us . . .*"

"*But I will tell you one thing, Randy. You have got a show you ought to broadcast into Europe and some of those countries overseas.*" Her televised face looked head-on into the camera now. "*And if my brother Clagg in Fayetteville is watching, I would just like to tell him not to take any wooden nickels. But you, Randy, you people have got a show here that they ought to . . ."*

"Christ-o, Fortunée," Biscuit murmured.

". . . broadcast across the Atlantic . . . and if a certain sailor boy named Marty is listening I just want to tell him my new home is Los Angeles, California, 'Where the Stars Are,' and I now live at 146 South . . ."

It was all over. PAIR-OFF! blinked into a tire commercial.

"Is that what I look like in real life?" She looked around at the four people in the room. In a dream, she rose from the carpet. She stepped between Biscuit and the refrigerator. "You saw me there. What is your opinion on the subject yes or no does television make everything look different?"

"Shit, man, what they ought to do," the man in the Hobie T-shirt was saying to Campbell, "is ask those poor dudes some batting averages or something they can get their teeth into."

"You looked fine, Fortunée." Biscuit was scraping plates. "Do you have to talk so loud in this small apartment?"

Fortune then turned to Milo and demanded his opinion; she asked him to choose on a scale one to ten, ten high, what number would he say she looked?

"Heavy, Champ. You walked off with the show. We're behind you all the way. You could go to the top, you know." He was peeling a pop-top ring off a can of beer. The spittle foamed up in the hole. "And, say, as long as you're asking—what was that bit again you said on the show about . . . you were a 'maiden'?"

"I do not see that it hurts to let people know a person is single and not married," she said.

115

" 'Maiden,' Champ, doesn't mean 'single.' "

"For your information, Mr. Beer, the people and 'the general viewing public' know what I am saying! They are not the ones to squibble about words even if you, Mr. Concussion Head, do like to do things of that nature!!!"

Biscuit came in, drying a fork. "Still and all, Roomie, 'maiden' doesn't mean single."

"It will mean what I say it means or be damned!"

" 'Maiden,' " Campbell said, "outdated as it may be—or as you might put it, 'in olden-days talk'—doesn't mean unmarried. 'Maiden' means you ain't neveh made it with anybody, Champ."

"You do not know olden-days talk or modern-day talk or anything under this sun because all you know, you, pudding you, is that you want ice on your privates and tell people you will do them favors that are not—and do not try to tell the rest of the world how to live her life!!!"

"Ruh-oomie!" Biscuit pretended to reel back. "Roomie, what are you talking, Roomie? Are you putting us on? You've never . . . ?"

While Campbell, incredulous, kept saying that Fortune was camp, "Still cherry? Camp. Very high camp."

"Roomie, no!" Biscuit squealed, and acting as if she tried to stifle the squeal, was turning to Cheryl. "Oh, Cher," she muttered, "this is too sad for words." Then to Fortune: "Oh, poor Roomie! No wonder you're so hung up! Poor thing, why didn't you *tell* us?" She was now sitting on the couch, slowly drawing her fingers through Campbell's hair. "Oh, Roomie, really? Oh, how tragic. Really? But, Roomie . . . why, you're almost thirty years old!"

"YES, AND AT LEAST I AM NOT *OVER* THIRTY AND

DIVORCED AND GOING ALL THE TIME TO MY BOY-FRIEND'S APARTMENT AND THEN *PRETENDING* I AM STILL A . . . MAIDEN!!!"

"Oh, wow, I don't believe this," said Cheryl.

Biscuit was on her feet now, her veins bulging. "You're babbling again, Chicken Little! But nobody's listening to you! But you listen to me and listen to me good, you f***ing little liar! I won't have you going around making up smutty stories. . . ."

"Oh, Christ-o, Biscuit," Campbell said. "Now don't *you* start coming on. Your bit is a good way to get a laugh out of consenting adults once or twice. But don't jack us, honey, don't jack us."

"My bi . . . ??? I am not a consenting adult!!! I am a little girl, Daddy!!! I AM 'LITTLE GIRL LOST'—YOU SAID SO YOURSELF AND THAT YOU WOULD TAKE CARE OF ME!!!"

"Oh, wow," Cheryl said. "Wow. I don't believe this. Wow."

13

"But that lucky old sun ain't got nothing to do . . . !" She was fooling around and waiting and watching. Now he was heading for the mailboxes.

Sliding—she was casual, to be sure—she arrived at her mailbox. She pretended to fight with the little door. He arrived at his mailbox.

". . . but roll around in heaven all day! Oh Lawd above . . . Oh! And good evening to you, Doctor. *'. . . can't you heah me callin' ' . . ."*

And where are you, at that time, standing in relation to Miss Besqueth's ex-husband—and we will talk loud on the "ex" part of that earmark . . . ?

". . . Work for my woman, toil for my kids . . . We professional types do not get to pick up our mail until the rest of the world has gone home or do you find yourself looking at the situation in that light of affairs, or not?"

"Yeah, I'll say," the dentist said. He was standing to her left. His mailbox was on the bottom row.

". . . sweat like the devil all the day . . . It is peculiar that I am running into you just now. Life is funny. Maybe you do not remember me, we danced. I thought maybe you were in an automobile crash. I was just on my way to Colonel

118

Sanders Fried Chicken or The Golden Cock to treat myself to a congratulations chicken dinner and him whoever else wanted to tag along. Anybody that wants to come, I am in the chips. My treat. Fourth of July. *Sweat like the devil all the day . . . !*"

He said, "What's the congratulations for?"

"Oh. My new position."

"Well. Congratulations." He polished his Polaroid sunglasses with his handkerchief.

In his car, a cavern, a casket that moves across the face of the earth toward The Golden Cock, it says "Polara." She is telling him that her new profession involves one of the major firms on the West Coast, that it means public contact and a person has got to "look sharp, be sharp. They are always watching to see—say, you have got a cuff button unbuttoned there—if a person has got that special way of handling a client." She tells him that her employers knew right away when she walked in for an interview that their product would be safe in the hands of a person with flair.

But her words are collecting about them both. They are floating and nestling about Skip Fritchey. He opens her door at the parking spot, and the piles of collected, fallen words tumble out the door like dry leaves and fall onto the pavement to blow away.

She tosses her fall over her shoulder and retrieves it, spreads it over her shoulder again.

She touches things on the table . . . salt shaker . . . ashtray, "Coors" . . . napkins . . . now the menu, flicking it with her fingernail, and her eyes ripple over the words there—what language is this? The señorita sleeves of the black dress brush across the tabletop. "*. . . roll around in heaven all day!*"

From behind his menu, he says . . . he asks: "You, say, you're really a . . . tense person, aren't you?"

"Tense? Ho ho ho. That is a 'scream,' like they say. You thinking I am 'tense,' but that is a good word for some people, do not get me wrong, you doctors know, yes, and what is your word for 'tense' is my word for my mind concentrating on my first big day tomorrow. Selling. 'Tense' could mean how am I going to sell the things when I get to the first door? And then I ring the doorbell. Here." She lifts the red sample case—or is it rising of its own?—to the table. She opens it. The crowded, wedged and busy little cosmetic samples gleam innocently. They speak, these little samples.

They are so small, so unassertive, they bother no one with their small size. It seems to her it will be necessary to defend them from the long gaze, the languor of this man who once took a wife. She will have to protect the little samples against someone who sloughs off wives the way a reptile shirks last season's skin. "Yes, true, they are little," she says now. "But you can see them real size here in the catalogue. Here is the catalogue. Now. You have got to put your hand out. Do that. Put your hand out." She removes a tiny tube of cream from the valise.

(Hold the . . . you did, at that time, actually tell him to . . . his hand out?

You just leave him to me, Bert. He knew it was all business and that Acting Forward might be A.F. in some situations but in others it is just business!)

The dentist places his hand on the table.

(Yes, but. Could you share with us at this time . . . sure he did not think you . . . making up excuses to touch him? If we are not out of line with that opinion?)

Fortune turns his palm up gingerly and squirts it full of hand cream.

(Beg pardon, Miss Dundy. But will you tell . . . *your* palm feel like when blah blah touches it in the middle with something? Do you not remember reading in That Book about . . . "erogenous zones"?)

She removes more samples from the red case, and the dentist says, "You've covered up the life line."

"Beg pardon?"

"You've covered up the life line in my palm. If somebody wanted to read it, he wouldn't be able to read part of the love line or the money line either, because of the hand lotion. Because of House of Circe."

"What? Well, yes, true, I guess I have gone and done that. But we will save that for a day we have not got House of Circe on our minds. They tell me, anyway, that a person needs a gypsy to handle that type of situation with the palms. Now, if you will just rub that in, you will notice a noticeable difference in your skin."

He says, "Why don't you do it?"

"Yes, and I am not a gypsy. They tell me you need a gypsy to handle that type of opinion."

Then he says, no, why doesn't she rub the cream in? is what he means.

"Yes, well, I am taking my samples out of my sample case. If you will just rub that cream in, I will tell you more."

Skip Fritchey massages, slowly, his own palm. . . . "So tomorrow's the big day? Apprehensive?"

"Yes, I have got a butterfly or two, like they say, about tomorrow, that you thought I was 'tense' about today. But I will do it. It is like the man at the interview says, I am a natural sales person. He could see I was the kind of person they were looking for, with my own terms and the own terms of the public."

"And what might those be?"

"Its own terms! What else!" She sweeps her tiny barricade of Circe samples off the table and into the red valise.

"Jumbo order of the chicken and two ice teas," says the dentist to the waitress. The woman turns to leave, and Fortune pops a toilet-water sample into her apron pocket.

"Compliments, House of Circe, honey," she says. "That is House of Circe . . . seer-see . . . *C-i-r-c-e*."

The dentist says, "You were saying about the public's terms."

"Look here," she says. "You be the customer. And I be me."

"Aren't you always you?"

"Yes, that is what I said!"

"Okay. I am the customer."

"And so you see, madam, after you use your Circe Cleansing Lotion, you have got your Circe Beauty Brace. Now a less 'classy' line of cosmetics might say 'astringent.' But I will give you this one piece of advice: Do Not Be Anybody's Fool. It is not the same. Ours, Beauty Brace, tops off your whole cleaning situation with an extra tingle. It draws those pores together smooth as a baby's skin, 'gets it together,' hah hah hah. Have you got yourself a pimple? Yes, I see you do. In the case of that pimple you might want to buy our Circe Medi-Cream for those devil bumps that pester us all from time to time throughout our lifetimes, short as life is. And, why, here, madam, here, hon, I forgot. Here you have got your Circe Tightening Grains. These get down in there. They rout out all that pore matter and grit and tighten those pores. Now. Are you going to a party? A wedding? Dancing! You want to smell just as nice as you look! Not one, but three! Spray tops and matching purse-size models . . . see it all here in the catalogue, Circe's 'Odyssey,' Circe's 'Lorelei,' and then here you have got your perfume 'knock-out,' Circe's 'Fatale.' Now: Let us try ourselves a squirt of our Number Four makeup base here. Let us put our Number Four right here on this side of your face."

She rubbed the makeup on his face and felt faint.

"I don't know," he says. "My husband is awfully big on the natural look."

Under her fingers, his light stubble is a thousand living things. . . . "Surely! And do you think he is going to know you have got our Number Four on! He will think it is your natural complexion! That is why I am here—to help you look natural!"

"Well," says the dentist, "just so I'm sure to look natural."

"You will look as natural as the flowers in May."

"He says nature knows best when it comes to putting a lot of gook on."

". . . 'a lot of' . . . ! What does your husband do?" Fortune says.

"He . . . he's a bookie."

"Yes, and would I try to tell your husband about books! No, I would not! So you tell your husband not to tell me about skin! Now . . . here is a mirror. Look. Even your skin does not know the difference from what is nature's handicap. Why . . . that Number Four is so natural, I will eat my hat

123

or your husband will be saying to you, 'Why do you look so natural tonight? I cannot get over how natural you are looking these days!'"

"Oh, you'd never hear him saying that. He's not one to dish out compliments."

"Huh! That is for sure! Why did you ever marry him?"

"We . . . we had to," Skip Fritchey says.

"Phooey! You have not got to do anything in this world you do not want to but be lonely! You should never have married a person that does not give you compliments. But it is too late now, never mind. Listen. Do you want me to tell you by what name we call Number Four at the plant? We call it"—she lowers her voice, leans—" 'Super-Natural.'"

"It doesn't say 'Super-Natural' on the bottle."

"Yes, of course not, honey! Of course it does not say 'Super-Natural' on the bottle! Do you think we at Circe go around giving out our code names to every Thomasina, Dixie, and Harriet? Well? Do you?"

"No," he says. "I suppose you Avon people do have your reasons."

"Avon? *A*-von? That one-horse outfit!!! We are HOUSE . . . OF . . . CIRCE—read! Yes, and I will pardon you this time, you have got kids and housework and do not get a chance to get out to the movies to keep you from being dowdy. If you did, you would recognize House of Circe right up there on all the stars' faces."

The dentist scrapes a fingernail across his cheek and examines his face in the mirror she is holding for him. "Hmmmm," he says. "This junk's so heavy I'd have to have a face-lift after each application. Say . . . did you say *'movies'*? You mean like Earl Westmore?"

"WESTMORE! *Westm* . . . well, yes, if you mean the

backwoods company that clogs the stars' pores, yes, all right. Please, can we change the subject onto something more professional?"

"I was about to say that myself. Zach'll be home in a minute and . . ."

Fortune says, "Madam, do you want to know a secret?"

"All right. I wouldn't mind."

"Around the plant we call this Number Four base 'The Liquid Makeup That the Stars Use.' "

"I'm glad to know that. Who uses it?"

"You mean to tell me," she says, "that you want me to tell you who uses it?"

"Yes," the dentist says. "You said the stars use it. Which stars?"

"You want to know right now? 'Right off the top of my head?' I will tell you one thing 'right off the top of my head.' We surely do not call our Number Four base 'The Liquid Makeup That the Stars Use' for nothing. For one thing . . . I heard that Loretta Young uses it."

She snatches the catalogue out of his hand and throws it in her sample case, snapping that shut.

The secret to all this selling and success, she then told him, was the sky because the sky was the limit.

He said he did not know it was that simple, but he was glad to hear her say it. "All slogans, is it?"

"Yes, and that is what I am saying! Yes! You have got to get in there with that human twinkle, that subterranean . . . that stops being just jars and creams and is a living product. I do not see why you try to say it is so hard to understand, with all these questions you are asking!"

He asked her then if he could ask only one more question.

"I did not say," she cried, "you could not ask questions! If the world went around not asking questions . . . yes, I did not say no!"

Skip Fritchey dabbed at a grease spot on his tie.

Or is he dabbing at her saliva?

Her head is pounding so hard, Bert. She is sure she feels her hair growing, her blood pushing her cells to their utmost . . . but hair, the experts say, dies, so maybe she is dying. . . .

She raises her cold drumstick to her front teeth and worries the crisp skin, waiting, studying the piece of chicken.

The dentist wiped his fingers on a paper napkin . . . the gesture was foreboding. "What if you find out," he says, "that all those people aren't going to buy?"

"I can see there is no sense talking to you! Now, I do not mean there is no sense at all in it. Yes, of course there has got to be some rhyme, some reason in talking to someone in the medical profession. . . ."

She told him then that her gums bled when she brushed her teeth, and Skip Fritchey said it was gingivitis and for her to massage those gums hard with Stim-u-dents.

14

Had it been two weeks since she had seen him, said that? Blah blah blah twelve thirteen fourteen days?

She followed him, watching him from afar.

The next time she saw him was when he went in Jeanine's apartment, E-32, and came out again . . . with Jeanine. Jeanine M. (for "Mercedes") Nicklaus. Jeanine, "common as dirt."

Another time she saw Skip Fritchey go in Jeanine's apartment alone about eleven o'clock one night.

She had gone then to E-32 and tried to listen through the outer brick wall, with a drinking glass. It had been the right wall . . . and maybe the right glass . . . but the wrong idea.

That night she telephoned Jeanine's apartment.

Jeanine answered. Her voice sounded pert . . . and powerful.

"Hello?" said Jeanine.

Fortune had wrapped some nylon stockings around the receiver. She said, in basso, "He is a devil sent to harm you," and hung up.

Later, toward dawn, she awakened and lay in bed thinking of what a foolish thing that had been to do. But the longer she lay there, the more her action appealed to her. So she got up and repeated it. This time the telephone rang several times, and Jeanine was groggy, cranky: "Yeah, what is it?"

"You have got your warning!" Fortune breathed heavily, sadistically into the receiver, big, heaving, dramatic gulps and exhalations.

"And just what warning is that?" Jeanine said.

"Zat ees none of your beezness. Eet ees too late, too late, too late!" And she hung up.

By that time, of course, she knew the dentist's schedule well. Once in the evening she passed his office and pressed her face quickly up to the glass. Nothing but a hall . . . leading somewhere. Where? And, too, during those weeks she was skulking, Biscuit came to her.

Fortune had been standing on the balcony, watching cars below arrive and depart. Biscuit had approached, chatty, homey, offering half of a Popsicle she was sucking. They leaned on their elbows a while over the railing, watching Dionysids go by. Then Biscuit, concerned, suggested that Fortune offer herself to Panchito, the little Villa Dionysus janitor, who came on Mondays, Wednesdays, and Fridays. Fortune would ask him to seduce her. ". . . as a favor, Rooms. As therapy for you. I'd let you have the apartment. I'd go to Mother's overnight. And you know, Roomie, they say those Latins really know their stuff. Now, wait a minute, I know what you're going to say, I know . . . but don't be put off by his height. Milo says that in Mexico the shorter a man is in height, the longer his doodad is supposed to be. And, wow, old Panchito'd probably be tickled to death. Poor

128

old greaser, he'd probably consider it social climbing. Even if it is you."

Then they watched television together, a late movie called *Till the End of Time* with Guy Madison and Robert Mitchum in uniforms . . . "Hi, soldier!" was all the world's name. And the girls at the ice-skating rink zipped across the ice, their little fannies darling, pleated, plaid . . . their heads flickering, their fannies bobbing harmlessly across the ice.

❖

She had been watching Panchito, she could see him in the doorway of the maintenance shed. He stood squeezing out a mop in his small—but strong!—hands. She turned back to the washing machine. A brand-new nightgown had faded. It tinted the rest of the wash a pale rose. When she raised her head, she saw Skip Fritchey go by the window of the laundry room, like a mistake. Instantly, she climbed into one of the large, empty dryers. She pulled the door shut after herself as swiftly as she could and turned her face away from the dryer's glass porthole. She had not even a moment to think why she had done such a thing when somebody opened the dryer.

It was the dentist. He said, "Are you dry?" and left.

15

And had you, at that time, given correct thinking to your decision?

I had, Your H.

Fine, Miss Dundy, it is "your funeral," like they say.

Oh, Your Honor?

Yes?

I will say one thing to you and our viewers at this time. And that thing is: When a person's mouth is bleeding, she will do things she would not do in other situations. And people like him are the first to know that, so do not you get smart with me, hear?

Fine, it is "your 'fyoon.' "

She caught him at his office, in his stocking feet.

He was at the back, past the chairs and glinting instruments. He sat at a desk with his feet up, and he was reading a book, *The Night of the Generals*. He wore a white smock stained with watery blood—was it blood?

She had waited until she saw his receptionist leave. She had waited, and she saw a light remaining.

He was very surprised, he had heard no one enter the

office, but he did not take his feet down from the desk. She stood in front of it, banging her purse against her thighs. He said, "Sit down." Cold steel utensils lay on white linen.

His hands certainly must always smell like mouthwash. And with that steel probe bearing on its tip a mirror the size of an eye . . . an eye-sized mirror which might very well be slipped on down a person's throat . . . way down, to look around down inside the area of her pumping, writhing soul.

Perhaps he was thirsty when he finished his day's work. It was now seven o'clock. He was no doubt thirsty earlier. There was an empty Coca-Cola bottle. He had finished off the last patient and come back here to this little room. He had walked . . . four, five, maybe six steps to the little refrigerator and reached inside for a Coke.

At some point he must have lifted the bottle to his lips and swallowed. That must be how this man took a drink of California beverage in private.

Then it was out and on its way—her question about where were Stim-u-dents sold.

He said he would give her some free packets he had.

Then he disappeared.

Now she had only a moment to alert The New Personality. Before he came back.

But here he was! Telling her to sit down . . . holding out the packets of Stim-u-dents . . . and the telephone began to ring. This was the signal for her eyelids, fingers, and her rib cage to fly off her body and take to the high roads out of the city.

Ringing, ring . . . he was gone again.

And this time she studied the colored snapshots under the

desk's glass top . . . and, too, there were the artifacts of his profession, the utensils.

A pair of shoes—so ordinary as to be almost arrogant—sat by the desk with a bottle of Shinola.

A five-by-seven color enlargement of Jeanine was under the glass. Someone had drawn a moustache upon her with two swipes of shoe polish.

"Sorry I took so long," he said when he came back.

He startled her . . . she had a moment of stylized fear, a feeling of being come upon. She imagined herself clinging upside down to the ceiling after the way of a cartoon cat . . . or even a fly.

"Glad to do it, don't mention it," he was saying. "Use those every day, much as you can, massaging those gums hard, and that will clear up your gingivitis."

He was removing his wristwatch now, rubbing his wrist. The expansion band had left it pocked. He put the watch, Bulova Tue 25, on the desk. These gestures of men! Always stripping off their watches or doing something to their belt loops! Or neckties, to their cuff buttons or cigarette lighters or wallets . . . canonizing car keys, ball-point pens, their pocket combs . . . combs more often than not slightly foul with use. Yet they had to be forgiven clogged combs. They had to be forgiven—they were men, were they not?—by virtue of being men . . . and, thus, ultimately pardonable, pardonable, pardonable. Nobody ever forgave women anything. Why was it women spent their lives apologizing? She did not see a fouled comb on the premises. But if she did, she would make it a point not to forgive the dentist for it. Those men movements of hitching at knees of slacks . . . shrugging into a jacket . . . rising, departing . . .

. . . a person could only flinch back and behold men, beings from an etherworld, a place male to its hot core. And now Skip Fritchey . . . he was an individualization from that etherworld. And now he was peeling off his wristwatch, putting it down . . . and rubbing the flesh of his wrist. "Sit down. Have a Coke."

"Charmed!" But it was no good. The New Personality had left her body, flown . . . the soul of popularity.

"You're all nervous again," he said.

"No, my gums were bleeding."

"More Coke?"

"Charmed."

He sat down then too. "It's very interesting that you live with Biscuit. I didn't know that."

"It is interesting."

"Yeah. She's quite a girl," he said.

"I have got to say yes to that opinion on the subject."

"Is she hard on you?"

"That depends on what is your opinion of . . ."

". . . 'hard on.'"

"Yes," she said.

"You're quite a girl yourself, Fortunée Dundy, Esquire."

"Yes, that is true. I will be leaving in a minute when I finish . . . this is my second Coca-Cola. I have got to be going along."

He said, "Selling?"

"Wrapping orders. Fixing the books. Tomorrow I cover Vernon." She rose abruptly and walked to a sink and washed out her Coke bottle and dried it on a paper towel.

"Sit down," he said. "Sold a lot? Tell me about your customers, your sky, your limit."

She sat, banging her purse. She told him about a woman in Alhambra who had answered the door with a boa constrictor wrapped around her neck. "It was a pet. I was thinking, 'Anything for a sale, anything for a sale.' That is my slogan—though I know you do not believe in slogans, that is mine. And I will always stand by it. She wanted me to touch it—have it around my neck—so I would know it was not slimy. I told her I would except I have always—got a match, by any chance?—always been a person very peculiar around my neck. Ever since I've been a little child. I could not, I told her."

"And what did she say about your neck?" he said.

"She said I had made it clear my opinion I did not want to touch the snake up against my neck."

"Then what?"

"Then she did not buy anything. She could not see her way clear to do it 'in the financial department.'" She was twisting the damp paper towel around the handle of her purse.

Skip Fritchey asked her then why she did not like anything touching her neck.

Just queer that way, she told him, ever since she had been a little child.

She looked down at the floor at a mound of damp confetti, the paper towel she had torn up. She cried out and fell to her knees—was she picking it up, piece by piece, or was she clawing the linoleum?—in search of a tunnel to the world of gnomes and moles . . . it would be wonderful to be a mole in the cool, uncritical soil. She was thinking very clearly. Her thoughts came to her in parody . . . weird hummings, but they passed on.

But she had picked up every piece of the shredded paper

towel. And he had watched her do it. He had not said, "Don't bother," although he had said something about her cleaning up her "disasters." She found the trash can and threw away the bits. His office, this whole place, smelled like death and unkindness.

"I came about my gums."

"I know," he said.

"Spitting blood."

"That's some purse you have there, Fortunée. What do you carry in there?"

To her astonishment, she had dumped the contents of her purse on top of his desk. "Then this I use to sharpen my pencils. A person has got to press hard on your order pad for good carbons . . . so I sharpen with this." She laid out her knife. "Do not jump back. It is only a kitchen knife. But a person never knows if someone is going to waltz up behind her in the night. She will be needing this. I read the other day a person about my age was found in an alley. Then . . . my house key. This Kleenex, of course, will not interest you even though it is clean. I carry it to blot my lipstick on. And speaking of my lipstick . . . here it is. One of many lovely colors I have got in my repertory. 'Mango Bloom' here by Circe goes with my blouse today. Tomorrow I might wear, say, 'Peppermint Plum,' according to your wardrobe puts your best foot forward. Here is a bobby pin with her rubber-tipped ends worn off, so out to pasture she goes . . . here is a hint: never use bobby pins with the rubber tips worn off. Breaks the hair 'like there is no tomorrow.' And any woman will tell you, her hair—we all remember Samson—is her crowning glory. Do you, by any chance, ever watch a television program, PAIR-OFF!? You would see the girls for Miss Mystery have split ends on their hair. Everything looks different on television. Now that little book you are looking at was a gift from a happy customer about four o'clock today. It is the smallest Bible in the world, they call it the Tom Thumb Bible. The woman bought some of our lilac guest soap. She had a shopping bag full of those little Bibles. I myself was on television once. She told me to carry the Tom Thumb with me wherever I went. And I would never want. I am carrying it."

"And do you want for anything?" he said.

"No. I do not. It is the smallest Bible in the world. You can see for yourself it fits in the palm of your hand. I like it because it is so little. That is some experience, being on television's PAIR-OFF! and interviewed. It is not really a whole Bible, like you can see when you open it up. Open it up."

He opened the tiny Bible. "Well, I've seen the Lord's Prayer on the head of a pin. But I must admit I've never seen a Bible this size." He read: "*Go to the ant, thou sluggard; consider her ways, and be wise: Which having no guide, overseer, or ruler, provideth her meat in the summer, and gathereth her good in the harvest.*"

"It is just the Twenty-third Psalm and six verses from Proverbs. But they call it a whole Bible just the same."

Skip Fritchey flittered through the tiny pages. "*And the light shineth in the darkness; and the darkness comprehended it not.*"

His voice had a pleasant, commanding timbre to it, although she, in her lifetime, had never cared much for the bossiness of the Holy Bible.

"She told me for headaches I can rub the Tom Thumb against my forehead . . . and for stomachaches. She even

136

said, hah hah, you can lay it on warts. No, of course, it is not a whole Bible." Then she showed him a pea-sized photograph of herself that had come out of a locket, and her eyelash curler, a package of Sen-sen, and her Social Security card.

He said, "Why don't you like anything to touch your neck?"

"Has not every person got his little strangenesses? Maybe you do not like, say, somebody touching, say, the center of your palm. Even an 'innocent tap.' "

He was standing with his back to her now, looking out the window. His hands rested on his hips. He seemed—how vulnerable he seemed! Stocking feet, back exposed . . . these aroused her. She watched his hair . . . an orderly thatch, it obeyed the back of his skull for a moment and then shagged down onto his collar. His shirt puffed out where it was escaping his trousers. And his slacks were tight now across his buttocks, as he shoved his hands deep into his pockets. Back and forth, he rocked on his feet. "Come here," he said. "What do you think of that view?"

He was looking at a large billboard with Little Miss Sunbeam chomping into a slice of buttered Sunbeam bread. "That," he said, "is my little peroxided Shirley Temple. Sometimes I change my clothes back here . . . take my shirt off, take a sponge bath in that very sink where you washed out your Coke bottle. I'll bet Little Miss Sunbeam watches me while I'm undressing. Nobody knows what a little voyeuse I have."

Fortune shot over to the doorway, certain that the word was a euphemism for his genitals.

"Yes, you know, you could close the curtains, you know!"

"Maybe I want her to watch me. Yes, I suppose I should close the curtains. But then she might watch you. Your apartment is in her sights."

"I always keep my curtains closed in that situation when I am dressing."

"Where're you going? Sit down," he said. "No, not there. I don't want you to wear that chair out. You already sat there twenty minutes."

"I did not. I only sat there three or five minutes! I do not see how I wore out your chair in that short time!"

"You did, but we'll let it go." He stood behind the chair and laid his hand on her head. Almost as if he were going to pluck it off her body . . . but softly. She flinched and rubbed with furor at her purse. "Chairs aren't living things," he said. "They can wear away and they never feel it at all. Now bodies . . . they do, they wear away."

"I will tell you one thing if you are interested! And that thing is I NEVER HEARD OF ANYBODY WEARING OUT A CHAIR IN FIVE MINUTES! IF YOU ARE GOING TO 'DROP HINTS' THAT I HAVE GOT TO PAY FOR IT, YOU HAVE GOT TO PROVE IT FIRST! Do not touch my head. I am funny about my head."

So he put his hand on the back of her neck and asked if that felt obnoxious.

"No! You act like I do not know about these things! I was not 'born yesterday.' And if you are going to start in on do I think your hand is awful, yes, I think the observation it has not got hair on it makes it like a woman's hand. Still, I do not hold that against you. There is none of us perfect in this world."

138

She was flaming . . . could have bitten his hand off. What would he do if her mouth opened the size of a bear trap and came down, CROMPCH, upon his arm? What a cannibal she could be . . . if he would let her. The jeopardy, his closeness intense as radar . . . his rhythm of speaking, of movement . . . his originality in gesturing . . . his perversity—all these things were fumes, dreams, they smothered her, stifled her.

He turned away now. His hands went into his front pockets. "What about you? You perfect?"

"Yes, I knew it! I suppose you are trying to say hints about the dirty lie of the Kleenex I lost out of the top of a certain bathing suit! While all along it was really only a paper ruffle that got torn up in the water! I have spent many hours going over that in my head! So do not think you can scare me with an inferiority complex!" She had lurched into a cabinet filled with rattling, clean, steel things.

"Jesus," he said.

"I know how you look for divorced people and the best people to . . . plug! And yes, I know a few things about you!"

"Oh, you do? Yeah . . . you probably do. Fine. Then tell me if you think I want to do that with you."

"I do! Yes, I do! Do you think I think you started fooling with my neck that it is my head and my neck you have chosen to fool with???"

"I do like your neck. But, as you guessed . . . I am principally a bust man. And, as you've told me all you have is a bunch of stuffing that comes out when you go swimming, there's not much else to say. Secondly, you talk so much, it gives me a headache. And thirdly, I don't like women walking unannounced into my office, telling me they know all about me."

"I happen to be a person that has got talent and poise!!!"

"Whoever told you that?"

"NOBODY! NOBODY HAS GOT TO TELL ME!"

"You're for real, aren't you?"

"*No, I am not! I am not anything you say!*"

"Why, then, did you come here? Faking your gums. You know what I think . . . you want some attention."

"I could kill you," she said calmly. "That would be attention."

He said, "Never mind. Okay, so you have your Stim-u-dents. Is that all you came up here for?"

Before she could answer, he dropped to his knees and put his hands around her ankle. Then he moved . . . slowly . . . and kissed the back of her knees, both knees, two kisses. He rose and whispered: "You have . . . a quality about you. You have stamina and imagination. Ah . . . and of what use are these things to me?" (He then said, almost to himself, "Indeed . . . indeed?") "Your neck . . . is soft . . . and secret . . . like the belly of a lizard. . . ." He sat down in his chair. Now he pulled at the tops of his socks . . . man-type deliberation. "I . . . look, I didn't mean to embarrass you." He gave a last tug and sat up. "But what is it you want?"

She had remained paralyzed . . . watching, flinching, mesmerized. She had borne those two strange, ritualistic kisses in turmoil and sadness.

"Ho ho ho," she said weakly. "That is a point to laugh about, your one about kisses. Kisses I can have any time I want them, from more persons than you have got hair on your head." All her senses fell in line. She was aware now of the man smell of him, remembered . . . of his white smock, faint perspiration and aftershave . . . and even the abstracts of his speech seemed to have a certain smell.

He said, "I don't really want to annihilate you. You can do that to the hard-ass women . . . and they say back, in their way, 'Oh, annihilate me.' Anyway . . . you wouldn't go around explaining the contents of your purse to the men you meet . . . and if . . . you could come out from those frills and furbelows and jumbo-jumbo eyelashes . . . but nobody really wants that. So you just stay there, where you are. Look . . . don't stand there like some Victorian heroine . . . because I'm not criticizing you, understand? I take it back, I take it all back. Your clothes are fine . . . your eyelashes are fine . . . I didn't mean anything. You're just fine."

He began to stroke her fall, as if it were real hair. He stroked it and sniffed it and ran his tongue through it.

She did not move. "See there!" she whispered. "You just pretend! You say something and then you say you should not say it!"

"Lots of people do that, Fortunée," he said.

"Not my kind of people! Biscuit and her boyfriend say things and he bites her, and the blood comes out on her lip!"

"What? Is that right? They do that? How do you know? Did you actually see that?" He drew away from her. In his hand was her false hairpiece.

He carried it away with him. He had removed her knife from her purse and cut her fall right off her head.

"Yes, they do! And you said you married her because she was horny!"

141

"Did I say that?" he said.

"You said 'horny.' 'Horny' was what you said!"

He stared at the fall in his hand, his face pensive, a mask almost grotesque. "Sweetheart," he said, "everybody around here is horny."

"I do not like that word! And a person of your profession that uses a low-class word . . . !"

"Oh, please," he said. "Don't be . . . shrill . . . you're all wrong to be shrill . . . life is shrill, but don't you be. . . ."

"Good-by! I will give you here what money I owe you for your Stim-u-dents!"

He said that would be four and a half cents. She snapped five pennies down on the desk, and he said he owed her a halfpenny change. "You do not owe me anything," she told him. "You keep the change! And anyway, they do not *mint* a half cent in California, do not think you can fool me!"

The dentist stacked the pennies carefully . . . he was removing two now from the stack . . . placing one over each of Jeanine's eyes. "Arf, arf," he said, rather to himself. "Arf, arf," like a dog. "Take it easy, Fortune. We'll see you around sometime."

She was already going down the hall, her high heels clicking on the linoleum, fast as castanets. She was lucid, bereft. But she was able to say, "My name is Fortu*née!* You see, you do not even listen!!!"

His voice followed her. "No. But I read," he called. "And the Social Security card you showed me in your purse said 'Fortune.'"

"YOU JUST DO NOT KNOW HOW TO READ FRENCH!!!"

❖

In the light . . . without the hairpiece, how naked, how ordinary she looked to the public eye. But the fall could burn in hell. And her own hair could just sit there on her head . . . a sparse garden of blighted corn. She went on down to the seaside, thinking, "The pier must be around here somewhere."

The pier was longer by night than it must be by day. She stopped in each pool of light. There was nobody on the pier.

Huge coins of light stretched on down the pier . . . ending in darkness and the sounds of the ocean . . . which were hard to distinguish from a film track.

Behind which coin of light in the dark stretches, where did the murderer with the knife await?

She began to walk. Well, the son of a bitch would meet his match tonight, people. The stabber would meet his match.

She continued walking until she did reach the end. And there was nobody. Her feet ached. She pulled off her shoes and threw them into the water below. But she was deprived of the sound of their disappearance. The waves crashed against the pilings.

Now that, Miss D., was a jack-ass thing to do.

Oh well, Bert, never mind.

The barnacles were welcome to those shoes. And the underwater life, the sea life could swim there and lay its eggs. The "Quali Craft" innersole would soon disassociate itself from the shoe. It would float out with the undertow. The fish—they could not read—would nibble the errant innersole, "Quali Craft."

Someone claws his way through the crowd. He reaches the opening and falls to his knees; strangled cry. The hair . . .

the gown . . . the body. "Limp as a glove." The eyes, people, are closed forever. And that heart that could not speak its mind . . . and that womb is waterlogged with the story of the sea! The womb . . . a giant saline douche rushes in . . . takes over . . . only Davy Jones will ever "know" her. But the sailor who won the anklet for her shouts to the heavens, We will drag the ocean floor from here to King Kong . . . prove I love you! Who . . . was she? someone asks from the crowd. Oh wow, katz and jammers, just some up-tight cherry jumped off the pier. What happened? Oh . . . someone annihilated her. But you did not answer my question—who was she? WHO WAS SHE? sobs the sailor. THE WOMAN I LOVE, YOU SONS OF BITCHES, AND IF YOU SAY ONE LOUSY WORD ABOUT HER I WILL CRAM YOUR LOUSY TEETH DOWN YOUR LOUSY THROAT. Oh, God, why? . . . A husky woman in the crowd steps forward, The Toklas, says her bowling shirt. I too knew her, says the shirted . . . I was the first in California to ever ask her for an official Date. Can the rest of you sons of bitches blah blah take your DataMate . . . blah blah your bigwig clubs, you know what "you can do with them." I did it blah blah simple as taking pie from a baby, did it over the telephone. Fortunée Dundy had a sort of *misterioso* you do not find at every five-and-dime. LET ME THROUGH! I am a doctor! Blah blah that pulse! Too late . . . an overdose of—stand back everybody!—of gingivitis. I am afraid the verdict is . . . no, God, please! Please, God, Take a Few Minutes to Read This Message Every Word Is Important to You! My Date's/Mate's race should be blah blah enjoy speaking before large gathblahblahs blah or at least one book or record club blah blah yes or no previous blah blah of the words listed below choose the five that you think best describe you.

And this is how she saw it:

```
       sensual        jealous
      athletic??      ??sociable
     political????  ????visionary
    punitive????????????taciturn
   submissive???????????funlover
   nervous??????????reckless
    grim??????????????????bold
     stubborn???????sexual
      curious??????stingy
       moody???????cruel
        talkative???sad
         optimistic
          lonely
           gay
            ?
```

16

At the May Day Beach Bash, she lies in the sand looking for him, waiting for him, berserk with suspense.

The road to hard-ass has meant new clothes, which she despises and wears. The words DIONYSUS WEST lie in black flocking upon her chest, over a Bacchus nebbish. There has been a volleyball game at sunset. Jeanine was not there, Skip Fritchey was not there. The sand is still warm.

Now it is late and growing later. People are settling into clusters around fires. They are peeling off into couples, rolling up in blankets, quiet as cocoons. Fortune unpacks the red valise and sorts out Circe samples by firelight.

She tells her friend: You be on the lookout, Bert.

Somewhere under that faded sun, this dawning moon— was there a moon?—somewhere in the Dionysid herd, she would be stepping, beg pardon, over a pair of legs . . . or turning a wienie . . . spreading out a blanket . . . something. And she would turn and see a pair of Polaroid glasses down the beach. They catch in each lens the moon, mirrored twice, two bright and nightly cataracts upon his eyes. He, wordless as the Grim Reaper, summons her . . . twink, twink, from each eye. He stands like Bela Lugosi, hollow, waiting, the strange, the depraved, the half-dead dentist, gentle as sex. These were part of her hallucinations as she distributed Circe samples.

✻

The very idea that she might come across him shot adrenaline into her throat. She began her circuit of the members, jabbing her Circe business card into the sand next to people rolled in blankets. Next to each card, she propped a sample.

She returned then and took orders. Jeanine and Skip Fritchey had not been at the beach party.

There was no moon. Multiple firelights caught the night surf . . . it broke in a long white lip, and behind her, the music of transistor radios rose.

Somebody, miserable and cheerful, stood at the fire. The sleeves of his sweatshirt were pushed up at the elbow. It said DY-GUY. When he turned, she read a homemade and wobbly "Phil" on the back; he had lettered his own name there in wobbly spray paint! Oh Christ-o. The man wore a Tyrolean hat. He held the hat on his head, as if there were a wind. He moved sand around with his toe. Scale, Miss Dundy? Oh, I would give him . . . a two . . . maybe two and a half, three.

She had begun to notice that the organization had its share of Phils; they came, they went, they—like she—remained . . . and they always found each other and put up with each other. While they talked over each other's shoulders, looking for other excitement.

And Phil—blithe, predictable, breezy—*He is just like me!* she thought—stood now at the fire. He swung his arms and socked his fist into the palm of his other hand, staring into the flames. He said a thousand stock phrases. Only ten min-

147

utes had passed. But Phil had shown himself to be a "Sorry about that" and a "Would you believe?" man. She wanted to slug him in the small of the back.

Glistening and shuddering, a hulk bounded up to the fire. He raked drops of water from his Tarzan's hair and he grinned. It was Harry, "Big Harry." "Hey!" he cried. "Why, it's Uncle Sam! How you doing, sweets!"

She was on her feet. "Good! Real good! And you—how are you doing there yourself, Harry! Harry, where have you been keeping yourself? I have not seen you around since the Fourth of July party way last summer—of course, I have not seen anybody much. What with my new profession and all. I have got . . ."

"That so?" Harry hunkered down now near the fire. He shook his wet vines of hair (a flying, salty drop tasting of hair landed on Fortune's lip) and hitched at his swim trunks.

Fortune squatted on the sand and watched him rip the key off his Budweiser, his body gleaming . . . a real temple of a man.

"Harry, no!" she said. "Not *swimming?* In the *dark?* In this *cold?* With those *sharks?*"

Harry was dreaming into the fire. He rubbed the hair on his belly thoughtfully.

"But, Harry, you are so wet! Here! I will dry your face!"

It went like this: Fortune had leaped at Harry, with her handkerchief. She was babbling (she knew) about he must take care of his skin. He should not allow water to dry upon it, and, of course, never salt water. Harry had blocked her hand with his beer-can arm, one jab, so swift that some of the beer sploshed out. Fortune had dropped like a puppet to the sand and began ironing her handkerchief on her knee. . . .

. . . Can you never shut up, Miss Dundy! Shut up!

. . . On and on she had talked. "You know, it is not going to do your skin any good . . . never let a single drop of water dry on *my* . . ."

"Yeah," said Harry, "you have super-duper skin. . . ." With one hand he bent double the empty Budweiser can . . . headed off down the beach, tossing it from hand to hand. . . .

She kept saying that what would she know about skin, she was only the major sales representative for one of the major skin firms here on the West . . . "What would I know? It is his skin that is getting ruined. . . ."

And Phil, unsummoned, said: "Ah, don't let it get to you. Those animals wouldn't know nice skin if they saw it. Do you enjoy your work with your company?"

"Animals?" she said. "Do not give me advice on animals!"

"I say, 'Do you enjoy your work?'" Phil reached up to anchor his hat.

"No, it is dumb. It is boring. Are you . . . cherry?"

"Oh, Highway Department now. I used to be a stunt man in pictures."

"And yourself?"

"Well, to tell the truth, I've got myself a background in pictures. The movies. I used to be in pictures."

"What do you do now?"

"Now? Me? Now I work for the Highway 'Dept.,' hah hah, of the State of California. I used to be a stunt man in the movies."

"Highway Department. How old are you?"

"'Old enough to know better. Too young to resist!' Hah had hah!"

What was the matter with his head? It was too oblong. The eyes were set mournfully close together.

She imagined Phil's head in a vice. He had grown up in a head-binding culture—Phil-san! Get back in this house! Where do you think you are going without your Bind-o-Brain! Our helmet produces the ideal head shape blah blah child and Pearl Buck blah blah Skulpt-o-Skull blah blah.

"Fifteen years," Phil was saying. "Ever see *The Alamo*? Or, try *Mission to Atlantis* or *Peril of the Pearl*." And there he was, trying to bend the beer can. He used two hands.

Then, "Busy?" she said. "No, I cannot say as Friday night I am 'busy,' if that is the word. I have got my profession, of course."

"You pretty good at it?" he said.

"Good? Yes, a person could say I am 'pretty good.' I was named Top Sales for my beat last week." (She had not shown the Circe newsletter to anyone. Her first whoop had died on her lips—they printed her at the top of the laurels list, all right: typographically: *Frotunée*.)

She stabbed a straightened coat hanger into a frankfurter. Phil was chattering happily; he shuttled back and forth from the flames to the mustard. Her wire with the wienie drooped into the flames . . . it bobbed, looked phallic to her.

✻

He would be in MEN.

The WOMEN side of the long, tiled restroom smelled of something universal . . . Sano-X, from bus stations, gas stations, cafés. WOMEN was empty.

150

She entered a stall and stood listening. From the MEN side she heard water running . . . the dentist. Running water . . . or *urinating?* Any moment now he would leave MEN.

She opened the stall door. She was startled to see a girl at the mirrors, combing her hair.

It was Jeanine.

But where had she come from?

"Skip?" Jeanine called now. "You still there?"

"Yeah," from MEN.

A single word, and it sizzled through Fortune's system like an electrode. *Yeah.* Sensuous, male . . . *yeah* had slipped into WOMEN through the ventilator shaft.

"Wait for me, hon! I'll be out in a sec!" Jeanine prinked at her face, made lips at herself in the mirror.

She did not know Fortune.

This was the first time she had stood so close to Jeanine. She pretended at her mirror and studied Jeanine's body in tight striped bell-bottom pants and a windbreaker. Beneath it her breasts rose, robust, no-nonsense. Jeanine stood on two staunch legs, fooling with her hair. Jeanine . . . looked very much like Biscuit Besqueth. Jeanine entered a stall and proved how mortal she was.

The dentist was waiting outside. He sat in a rectangle of light from MEN. He spoke first. "You got here pretty speedy. Only a few minutes ago you were down roasting hot dogs."

"Beg . . . ? Oh, it is you, Doctor!"

"My alter ego."

"Yes, and I can use the toilet if I want!!!"

"You left your hair in my office last month," he said. "Coming back for it?"

"You are a devil. I do not like you. I do not see that some-

151

body of your profession should do that with a knife to me, to my hair!"

But Jeanine came out of WOMEN. She clambered onto his shoulders and cried Giddiyup! He rose with her, bore her away; she was squalling, Help! Help! I'm falling. Where Skip Fritchey had been sitting, his spirit hung over the sand . . . occult, menacing. MEN said the sign. Through these portals pass MEN. MEN for you, and MEN for me. MEN for today and MEN for tomorrow. Right up that street, around that corner, through that door marked MEN. MEN with penises like cartoons, jutting out like frankfurters, drooping and confusing genitalia that looked like newly hatched squabs. MEN with penises, MEN with promises. She went back inside WOMEN to use the toilet. There was a big janitress with L.A. Park and Recreation embroidered across her bosom. She was banging in the stalls, slogging her mop across the floor.

Fortune had not seen the janitress enter WOMEN.

How did all these people . . . slip by her? What was that . . . an omen? Who was the janitress? Speak, scrubwoman! Was she a messenger . . . ? Did the janitress blah blah a note in her pocket? My darling Fortune, your knees, your hair, let me enter you, let me stroke your spine with the knife you left me. Let me love you and stroke you and make everybody forgive you! Blah blah the sadness and weakness and the wetness you felt between blah blah blah your dumb jabbering heart when you saw me sitting in front of MEN! I understand. I understand. I know these things. I will wait for you. You will know me. I am the one waiting in the light from MEN. We will kill Jeanine and go away together, you and I.

She left WOMEN. She had not used the toilet. It would

152

have been too embarrassing . . . with the janitress there listening.

And outside Skip Fritchey's spirit remained on the sands, silent, full of fatal rites, fatal bliss.

Still another daydream burned behind her eyelids. Along with newer, unsorted realities. The pinpoint lights of tankers passed ominously offshore . . . there was definitely no moon scattered on the water in broken chips . . . a moon that lighted her way to those ships. Packed with sailors . . . teeming, strapping, randy, bored to bits, playing cards under their Raquel calendars. (Samuel! His name made her weak.) She gets a rowboat somehow . . . rows out there across the oil slicks. A ladder is lowered. The guys are sprawled around on their bunks. Yowee! Woman flesh! I saw her first! No, me! Cigarette, luscious? Beer? Move over, you maggots, let the lady blah blah! Sing something blah blah, honey! Blah blah blah blah in your repertory? "Blue Moon?" "Moon Over Miami?" "Shine on, Harvest Moon?"

❋

Phil lay on top of her on the sand. He kneaded her. "Oh, Gawd," he said. "God-God-God." Then he told her they had just "faked intercourse."

"We had our clothes on," he whispered. "So it is not a sin. Nothing happened. I just made a mess in my . . . oh, Gawd, I love you! I love you, Fortunée! I wanted you all night!"

"I love you too," she said. "But I do not want you. You are not what I have got in mind at all."

He was saddened, cut, by her words. "Sorry . . . about that," he said.

He had tried to start a songfest around the fire at the

beach party. "Come on, everybody, join in!" he cried. "Let's hear it! Hit it, Fortunée! *Shine on, shine on, Harvest Moon. . . .*" But people were rolling up blankets and wadding bun cartons into the coals. Fortune and Phil stood by. They tried to harmonize then on "Heart of My Heart." They stopped and started and told each other the other would have to begin in a higher key.

Now everyone was gone, and she and Phil lay next to dead fires.

Her body ebbed and throbbed like a dull heart and she lay very still and sullen. She thought about the nauseous parody of lovemaking.

She lay silent, Phil's rancid breath upon her neck. She was thinking about the shape of his face and head.

"Why so quiet, kid?" he murmured. "Didn't know yourself, did you? Ah, come on, buck up! You were 'jest a-doin' a-what comes natcherly!'"

17

She lay on her bed, eyes closed. A single bite of American cheese idle in her mouth.

From the living room: "I . . . *SAID:* RUSTY . . . CALLED!!!"

Biscuit's hair was greasy. Her stomach hung out over her bikini panties. The elastic bit into her thighs and buttocks. "D'you hear me, Fortunée?"

"Yes." She swallowed the cheese. "My, that is a pretty voice you have got on this evening."

"RUH-HUS-STEE, YER BULL DIKE KELL-ED YER!!!"

"And your lip. It is swollen up again. It looks like somebody bit it, drew the blood."

Biscuit's anguish was two days old.

Campbell was going to propose marriage. Biscuit had been insane with euphoria. She pirouetted, hugged pillows, bellowed "Get Me to the Church on Time." She had that day put the final black and white cushion in Campbell's apartment. "Eight solid months of redecorating! Done!" She had wrapped Fortune up in a bear hug and swept her out of B-12. Hand in hand, they bolted across the courtyard to A-36. Biscuit flung open the door—"Ta da! Ta da ta daaaaa!"

—upon the "chess-set motif": mostly giant black paper flowers and citrus crates painted white, stacked as coffee tables, shelves, and "a settee."

In their beds in the dark they giggled like little girls and discussed colors for bridesmaids' dresses. To celebrate the apartment, Campbell was taking Biscuit to dinner tomorrow at Trader Vic's. But, more important, he said, to create "a special occasion, Roomie, 'in a special atmosphere to make a very special offer.' (Oh, and I've got to show you the silver pattern in the July issue!) 'Special offer,' he said and swatted me on the hiney. Oh, men! Christ-o, what would we do without them? Oh . . . poor Roomie . . . but we'll still be neighbors! Fortunée, I've been worrying about you a lot. You know I love you, don't you? And I've been thinking . . . listen, Roomie, tell you what. We're going to take care of your little hang-up, yes, we are! We'll get Milo to ball you! He'd be great for your first time—he's handled lots of cherries (as a matter of fact, I'm looking forward to our wedding night myself). Because, wow, Rooms, I don't think you should let another day go by, you know?" She had hurled her stuffed animal against the Venetian blinds. "Wheeee! He said he wanted something more stable in his life!" She snapped on the light. "Oh, Barbar! Did Mommy hurt you?"

She then wanted Fortune to telephone Skip Fritchey.

"Right now. You simply make like, you know, you're calling up to say hi. And then you casually let it drop. You know, 'Hey, Skipper, I guess you've heard the big news.' He says, 'What news?' You say, 'My roomie's getting married.' Or, no—better—the way *you* do it: 'Hi, Doctor, and how's yourself?' And eks-cetera. Then you hand the phone to me so I hear how that bummer news grabs him. I've got the

156

number here . . . Christ-o, he's still living in that dingy little pad we had over in South Pas. You say, 'Hi, Doctor . . .' Oh, Jesus, talk about a bummer! This bastard's going to fall off his chair. . . ."

"I think for this situation you best break the news your own self."

"Nope. I want to hear his reaction. He's sure as shit not going to give it to me straight to my face. I mean, you think he would give me the *satisfaction?* So you call."

"No. Thank you, anyway."

"Roomie, don't start that shit, come on, please. Not when I'm so happy."

"I have not got any reason to be calling the dentist!"

"You do too! Didn't you tell me the other day you were friends with him? I asked you, and you said, 'Oh, we're just good friends.' "

"I did not mean what you want it to mean right now." She had gotten out of bed and gone into the kitchen to pretend to look for food. "I would never in two thousand years call him up. So take that out of your head! But, anyway, even if I did, he would know right off it was you put me up to it to let him know."

Biscuit followed her and stood in the kitchenette, hands on hips, naked. The glass doors to the balcony reflected her dark pubic V, her two breasts hanging like hounds' ears. "Don't be an imbecile!"

"Beg pardon?"

"Christ-o. Oh, all right, you're not an imbecile."

"I am not an imbecile, Beverly."

"Then why won't you call him up?"

"On account of it is not my concern. And on account of

I do not want to do it!" She stood now lining Circe samples along the sink, polishing the little bottles. "Why do you not ask one of your friends to call him and say the same information you just told me to say?"

"Because . . . " For a moment Biscuit was artless . . . almost poignant. "I don't have any friends. Who would I ask?"

"Well, my, you have got Cheryl," Fortune said. (She was distracted by Biscuit's naked body, reflected in the glass doors . . . it was opaque, shadowy. It aroused Fortune—she imagined it her own body parading in front of someone who loved her. She remembered dancing once, nude, in front of the mirror when she was in high school . . . she had pretended she was in a cabaret in front of sailors. Bert used to remind her of this later: You used to make those swabbies "hornier and hornier," did you not, Miss Dundy? he would say.) "Yes, why, you have got Cheryl!"

"Cheryl . . . ? Now, don't go around calling me a speed freak, Fortunée! Or telling people I'm buddy-buddy with a bunch of wrecks!" Then Biscuit had banged all the cupboards and pulled all the drawers out. She hurled them on the floors. Forks and pans and pancake turners clattered across the kitchenette. "All right, I won't ever ask you for another f***ing favor as long as I live!!! I'll call the bastard myself, we're good friends." She called then.

Jeanine had answered and Biscuit asked for ". . . my ever-loving ex-hubby . . . Hi, Skipper-Dipper, hi, big boy . . . sounds like from the background sounds that Jeanine is fixing you our class recipe for chicken cacciatore . . . but save some room for wedding cake. . . ." And then that he and Jeanine would get "a ringside pew . . . Thanks . . . I know we will . . . Yeah, catch you later too."

Biscuit snapped off the lights and whipped back the sheets of her bed.

After a few minutes' lying in the darkness, Fortune said: "You see there! He did not want to talk to me at all! Or he would say give my best to your roommate or something along that nature!"

Biscuit said nothing for a long time. Then: "Hey, Roomie?"

"What?"

"That Jeanine. What a smug little pig. Hey, Roomie . . . how'd you like to give me the happiest wedding present ever? Take Skip away from that smug little pig. Hey . . . Roomie? Think you can do that? Hey . . . ? Sssssst? Fortunée? Roomie, you awake?"

The following night Biscuit had come in at three A.M., from Trader Vic's. She had turned on the light and hurled herself upon Fortune's bed. She screamed that she was going to kill herself.

Campbell, in wanting something "more stable" in his life, had invited Biscuit to live with him.

"Just like that! Shack up with him! Oh, the bastard! The humper! The baller! *The dreamer!!!*" She groped her way to the telephone. "Fortunée . . . dial this number . . . can't even see to . . . Oh, Mommy! Mommy! Help me, someone!" She snatched the receiver out of Fortune's hand.

As she placed Biscuit's Trader Vic's orchid in the toothbrush glass, she overheard her tell San Marino that tomorrow she would be dead.

*

A tiny woman, tanned, platinum-haired, flew in the door.

It was evening and Fortune lay collapsed on the couch amid her Circe samples.

The woman pitched her mink stole—hot as the weather was getting to be—onto a chair and began pacing the apartment, smacking her hands together, tapping her cigarette in various ashtrays.

Biscuit, drinking Scotch, had advanced on Fortune. She crossed her arms over her chest: in the past, this signal meant "Beat it."

Now Fortune pretended not to notice. Now she was at the table, scribbling Circe orders. She clipped and tied. She addressed Biscuit's mother, without being introduced. "Yes, sir, San Marino is quite a place. I get out there a lot with my profession."

(. . . which was *almost* true.

What was more true was that California was changing. Take the bus drivers. Huntington Drive: she had boarded and paid and settled into a seat behind the driver. She had smoothed her skirt a thousand times as she glanced across the aisle. You never know what kind of people buses may bring into your life. Finally, even though the sign over his head had said not to annoy the driver with unnecessary talk (*unnecessary* talk, indeed! Why did the world always tell a person not to do the thing you most need to do?), she spoke to him. Why let a sign always try to be the boss of you? She said to the driver, "If you saw one, would you know the mark of a born salesperson?" He had thought she said Salisbury. Then Mrs. Hempie got on the bus. She wore one of those shoes with the giant sole, an "elevated" shoe. She swung it down the aisle and plopped down next to Fortune. In her shopping bag she had carried hundreds of paper cups and napkins that said "Maxine and Bill." Her daughter was getting married in the back yard. Fortune had said, for openers, "No chance that sole wearing out on *that* shoe, I hope to shout."

Mrs. Hempie had chuckled and shifted her shopping bag into the seat next to her. "Oh, you'd be surprised. In time it does get itself scraped down on one side. Gets wore down, you know."

"Well, there's an old Indian saying about a person should walk a mile in the other person's shoes—I would not want to do it in yours! No, I would 'not want to be in your shoe,' like they say. All the same, it looks a sight more down to business than these high-heeled babies I wear. I would get myself something more soothing if it was not for my profession. But they are 'swanky.' And you know what they say: a person's career comes first. You have got to plant that best foot forward and that foot has got to be looking chichi when you have got the kind of profession I do."

"What d'you do, darlin'?" Mrs. Hempie had asked.

"Public relations and personal contact."

"Oh, you don't tell."

"I hope to shout. Say, what would you say is your opinion on the subject what is the mark of a born salesperson?"

"Of a born salesperson?"

"Yes. What?"

"Well . . . best foot forward, like you said."

"I am in the selling and personal contact line. Here. I am going to give you some free samples. *Listen, do you want me to tell you what a woman said to me about her garden walk?* Oh, 'wow,' never mind, but you would not *believe* how some people throw *simpático* out the window when they see a professional person walking over a garden with a red lizard sample case in her hand!"

A policeman, cruising by lazily in midafternoon—that is,

161

he had *seemed* to be cruising—had stopped his patrol car. She was squatting on the edge of a lawn . . . a Spanish colonial house . . . replacing some Circe samples in her kit. No, Officer, she had not known that the good people of San Marino could, would . . . *prosecute* . . . door-to-door people. Had . . . someone reported her? Well, yes, it seems he had received a call. No . . . no, he wouldn't run her in. Not *this* time. So that had been San Marino. Brief. Elite. Hot. Green. Sleek. A place of wicked, comely gardens with high blood pressure . . . colored shade . . . the colors of the flowers rising into the vines and trees . . . fat gardens, ornate, smug, ruddy . . . where the pollen smothered even the insects . . . and the flowers stood quiet, like bands of sullen, solemn gypsies . . . the fuchsia, the gladioli, the zinnias, the snapdragons, the roses, marigolds, and chrysanthemums and mimosa and honeysuckle perspiring. . . .

. . . That had been San Marino. Rich. Hot. Green. Specious.) "Yes, sir, quite a place."

Mrs. Besqueth turned. Her contact lenses, two audacious emeralds, swam on top of her irises. And what was it Fortune did? she asked.

"I told you, Mommy. Fortunée peddles makeup, door to door."

"Try Circe's 'Odysseus' aftershave for your men!" She popped a sample into the woman's hand.

Mrs. Besqueth said, "I'm sure Daddy'll love this."

"No. He does not like my brand," said Fortune.

"She's talking about my father, Fortunée."

"Beg pardon, beg pardon one thousand times. A person sometimes has got a problem on her hands keeping the Daddies straight in this world."

162

Biscuit dipped her finger in her Scotch and slowly flipped some drops in Fortune's face. "Hah . . . hah . . . hah. Very funny."

"She means Milo," said Fortune.

That set Mrs. Besqueth off. She paced the room. "And here's what we'll do, honey. You let him know there are other fish in the sea. And that if he stalls *too* long, well, happy landings, Mr. Milo Campbell!"

Biscuit sploshed her glass down on the table. Fortune picked her receipts up and dried them on her peignoir and went on writing. "Fortunée, I hate to be rude, dearie. But either Mommy and I talk here or we'll have to go to the rec hall for privacy. . . ."

In the bedroom, Fortune pretended to close the door.

"You've simply *got* to put a little scare into him," Mrs. Besqueth was saying. "Isn't there some boy in the club here you could go out with once or twice? To let Our Friend know his girl can bring down a good price on any man's market! Isn't there someone? Let's think."

"Sure," said Biscuit. "Skip Fritchey."

"Oh no, now, let's not go into *that*."

"Christ-o, would that ever be a bummer for Milo! That'd get some action out of him!"

"That's it," said her mother. "Now you're getting the idea. But let's think of some nice boy. Why don't we go through your little club catalogue thingy and see who comes to mind? Here . . . look at this boy. His picture looks awfully sweet. Know him? 'Charles . . .' Oh-oh. Sounds Mexican. Do they let Mexicans in this club? 'Romero.' Charles Romero. My . . . and he's so blond!"

"Oh, shut up!" Then Biscuit began to weep. "Oh, Mommy,

it's all so . . . unfair! He used to love me so much . . . he still does! And that apartment—you should have seen him around there . . . he loved the motif and helped me and . . . oooooh! What is he waiting for? Oh, *do* something!!!"

Mrs. Besqueth began to cry also.

Then she said the one important thing for Biscuit to remember was: Do Not Give IT to Milo. That very well may be what he is after. And as soon as he gets IT, then he really *will* stall. "After all, darling, why should he marry merchandise he himself has already soiled? Why should he buy what he can rent? Oh-oh, let's see how long our Mr. Campbell can hold out. You make it very clear to him that The Little Extra comes in the package deal, you're saving the payoff for the wedding night. You tell him this—say, are you listening to me?—tell him: no wedding, no bedding. Get it? Say . . . come here, Bevvie. Over here into the light . . . you look a mess, your eyes are red, your pupils are all dilated —my, they *are* dilated!—you have dark circles. . . . We've got to get you back into your old pert self. I'm going to call for a metabolism for you with Dr. Krohn. . . ."

Fortune burst into the room, punching a pencil behind her ear, fussing with her peignoir, looking for Quaker Puffed Rice. "And that is just what I have been telling her! She came in here with her lip swollen up and would not trouble me about it. She did not want to worry any of us, you know."

"Saaaaay," said Mrs. Besqueth, "I *thought* there was something funny about your mouth." She followed Biscuit, who walked away, screwing the cap on the Dewar's bottle. "Come over here in the light a minute, baby. Let's have a better look at you."

Biscuit had whirled away into the kitchenette. She began slapping dishes from the drainer into the cupboard. "Oh, nothing. Shut up! Milo braked, and I hit the Morg's windshield. And as for you, Fortunée, I don't see that I have to explain every little bump on my face to you! So don't go around freaking my mother out about it!"

"Oh, beg pardon, beg pardon. I only meant it looked to me that some person had maybe bit you on the lip or something. Hard enough for blood to come . . . or something of that nature. I did not know it was only a windshield. I thought some person had come up and bit down real hard on your . . ."

"Oh, F*** OFF, you!!!" Biscuit said.

Mrs. Besqueth was already on her way over to "take a look at that lip." She followed Biscuit around the kitchenette, dodging Fortune. Biscuit pulled all the drawers out and hurled them on the floor. She picked up a long barbecuing fork.

"But I suppose if a person thinks about it," Fortune said, facing Biscuit's approaching tines, "a car windshield has got its ways of biting."

Mrs. Besqueth was saying, ". . . knew it! I knew it! I told you you were working too hard on that apartment. . . . I suppose you think you can redecorate at night on top of eight hours at a desk at Creighton-Stapleton? You think all this labor is good for your female organs, I suppose? We aren't built for mining coal, you know. Let horses mine coal."

"MOMMY!" shrieked Biscuit. "My organs don't give a shit! It's my mind that gives a . . . Mommy, I'm going out of my head! He's destroying me!!!"

165

Mrs. Besqueth . . . tamping out a cigarette, walking now . . . "Well, you just hold out for the wedding night."

"Moth-*er!*"

"Oh, pay me no mind! You people just go right on with your chat. I am a cornfield without ears. I am busy here putting my Circe orders . . . I am like our famous monkeys, hear no evil, speak no . . . let me see here, Mrs. C. Marsh in Santa Monica wanted our Circe Bath Powder. . . ."

18

(The telephone is ringing. Adrenaline. Hello. Adrenaline subsides.)

"Yes, this is Fortunée Dundy."

"Hiya, toots! Prince Philip here! Get your forty winks?" He laughed zanily.

And so on . . . chuckling, pauses, vaudeville. (While on her end of the line, for the practice of it she remained a little bit cold, a little bit hard-ass. But she called him "darling." To confuse him.)

The telephone had jolted her awake. A single shaft of late afternoon sun struck her face. Between rings, the apartment was sinister. She was lonely for Biscuit. All the curtains were drawn. Outside, like one human body against another, the sun pressed up against the wall of B Wing. Heavy, flat, the sun waited outside, an old man peeping, eavesdropping, playing with himself.

She yanked open the curtains. The little Miss Sunbeam billboard grinned into the living room . . . sinking her teeth into that buttered bread . . . as if it were a piece of somebody's flesh!

(All night long they had gone to the movies. A midnight-to-dawn special at the Big Sky Drive-in in Monrovia. Then they ate breakfast at Pancake Heaven. At eight A.M. Phil had deposited her and his single rancid kiss at B-12's doorstep.)

She sprinted down to the Hot-Deli at the Jiffy Center. A windstorm had come up; it was thundering. On the way back, a kid on a bicycle nicked one of the soup cartons out of her hand. At B-12, she threw the cartons' contents into the pans on the stove. She warmed up the dinner and tossed into Phil's soup: Nu-Gro plant-food crystals, a couple of Biscuit's Ovulen, a few drops of Circe's "Lorelei."

He tipped his hat all during dinner, complimenting her on each dish. He winked at her. His praise ran out of his mouth into the soup . . . jumped back up into his mouth from the macaroni and cheese. He winked at her so often, it seemed like a tic. "You sure can cook! You cooked up a storm here! What do you think about marriage? Just in general?"

It began to rain, hard. The leftover Jell-O melted in its cartons. The hailstones pelted the glass doors. At some point Biscuit and Campbell blew in the door, their eyes too bright. The electricity blew. The four of them sat in the dark. Phil suggested ghost stories.

He told one that began: "Wait'll you hear this, it'll curl the hair right off your head . . . and so during the filming of *The Peril of the Pearl*, the stunt man went down, down, down into the glass tank . . . cameras rolling . . . the giant clam opens its jaws and . . ." It ended: ". . . pried open the jaws six years later? The poor schmuck's head! Laying there! You guessed it—pearlized!" Fortune's ghost story was about a nurse in the Mayo Clinic. About some prankster orderlies and a cadaver's arm and a light-bulb cord. And later the nurse being found under a bed, chewing on the arm, her hair snow-white. Biscuit began to sob. And Fortune added, "No, now wait, Beverly, this is not the end. The end is that a wonderful doctor named Dr. Port Porter came along and went into her cell. He said, 'Now do not be afraid, little nurse. Everything is going to be Roger.' And he took the dead arm and he showed it to her. And he said, 'Now, is that arm anything to be afraid of? It is only an arm. It cannot hurt you at all. It is dead.' And he, Dr. Porter, even took the arm and rubbed it against her neck . . . she had been particular around her neck before. 'You see there,' said Dr. Porter. 'Dead arms are not living things. They cannot hurt you at all.' And they kissed and later they got married." The lightning showed Biscuit and Campbell by the glass doors, silhouetted in an electric frame. Campbell sat in a chair. He was bracing his heels against the rug, arching himself upward. His head was thrown back. Biscuit stood behind the chair, her hands on it. Her elbows were in the air like skeletal wings. She was kissing him. In that single instant of lightning, they writhed, joined like two huge insects in a joint death throe.

Phil saw it too. He whispered, "You know, I *thought* I saw something."

Out in the rain, the hat blew off Phil's head. A lump, a goiter affair, gleamed high on Phil's forehead. But she told him not to feel bad. She added a story about a Buddha in a pawnshop. The pawnbroker said the high, long head of the Buddha meant there was an extra set of brains. This gave the Buddha his extra wisdom.

They were sitting in a coffeeshop somewhere on Melrose Avenue . . . or some other avenue, maybe; some other boulevard . . . Guggy's. They had begun to talk about Biscuit and Campbell. And then about group sex and sodomy and Hollywood and people Phil said he knew. "Oh, you ain't seen nothing, chickadee," he told her. Phil said that, in particular, one of Hollywood's most hallowed and bull-necked male stars would begin by watching men—over forty years old—urinate into goblets. No, no names, please. A four-time Oscar nominee. Someone, in fact, for whom Phil stunted *a nightmare of a free fall from a two-hundred-foot cliff. And into boiling rapids.* Oh, no, peaches; again, please, no names. Goblets, right. Six of them. In a circle.

"Have you done those matters?" Fortune said.

"Hey, now!"

"Come on, Phil. 'Get off it.'"

"Look, my sweet . . . there's a lot you don't know about this town!"

"Does the Highway 'Dept.' know about this?"

". . . and about . . . about the way you can . . . you can get sucked into deals you don't even . . . ! Baby, it's a ve-ry weirdo business, the pictures . . . and . . . and . . . don't think I don't regret . . . ! Aw, baby . . . sweetie, don't be so hard on me!!!"

19

"Our Wedding" says the white and gold album.

And such photographs! The sun-streaked, the unholy and coltish groom! The sun-streaked bride! Children of the sand and foam in ducktail haircuts and pageboy bobs! His lips upon hers! Hers upon his! Who are these two nineteen-year-olds in this still-life kiss, sealed in black-and-white matte finish? Who plunges that blade into that tower of frosting and sugared bells? (They stuff each other's mouth as if the cake is life itself!) Billowy that veil! Snowy the gown . . . the tulle gushes out of her body like Niagara Falls. Her bridal bouquet hangs suspended in the air, some lacy UFO. Underneath? An eddy of bridesmaids' fingers . . . up, up, up, they twitch and ripple upward toward the bouquet. They are flagella, a thousand fingers, a sea anemone!

Fortune squints hard at the dentist, sneezing champagne all over his tuxedo. *Some* photos.

"What do you mean, you 'can't do it,' Fortunée?" Biscuit walked into the living room, her two tired banana breasts joggling. She stood and examined the stretch marks running over them in white rivulets. "Look. All you do is invite him over here for a drink. Then you go tell Milo B-12's closet door is stuck and needs fixing. He still has a key. Then you split."

Campbell had a new girlfriend.

Biscuit had been in San Marino in bed, under a sedative, following this news.

Now she was back. She looked only a little hollow, slightly grainy. She talked to herself. Muttering obscenities . . . she studied her reflection in mirrors, stainless-steel coffee-pots, in spoons. She pulled wanly at her hair and touched her breasts in consternation. But a stout shadow of determination followed her.

Her plan was to get Campbell "back." She returned from San Marino with the albums from her and Skip Fritchey's wedding. When the jealous Campbell saw them out on her coffee table . . . and the dentist himself in B-12, he would drop Nina, "the little whore copy typist" from his advertising agency. And he would return to Biscuit.

"You get the dentist over here yourself if you are so hot under the collar to have the dentist over here!!!" Fortune said.

"You'll be sorry." Biscuit whirled away and telephoned Campbell's apartment for the fourth time that evening. She asked for the man who sold Pudding Tain. She slammed the telephone down, gagging. ". . . balls on that bitch! How dumb does she think I am?!!! I *heard* him in the background playing his crappy little tape for his shitty little pudding! *'Caesar's Discovery! Imperial Flavors! When at Home Eat As the Romans Did!'* Have you ever heard such a bunch of *shit?* Roomie, he can't do this to me! Help me! Oh, why do men change? They're one thing when they're getting their ass and then when . . . oh, Christ-o, just try to get some *responsibility*—what're *you* looking at?—walk around her like some f***ing goddamned white dove! Oh, you think you're so f***ing superior, don't you?"

Fortune said that yes, she did have that opinion of herself, but any way a person cared to look at it, she would never go telephoning a man's apartment, ". . . and *chasing* him after he is telling me in no uncertain negative acting with other people that he is no more interested in me than the man in the moon!"

"Yeah," Biscuit said. "And the man in the moon would ball you if he got the chance too!"

Fortune said, "Yeah. And he would not get the chance!"

Biscuit careened away, tears in her eyes. She grabbed Fortune's hand. "Listen . . . Roomie. He's destroying me . . . but he doesn't know how happy I can make him! I'd, Christ-o, I'd move into that apartment just to be *near* him . . . I'd do anything. (Oh, I could take those demo tapes and cram them up Nina's little . . .) Her, Nina, he's making love to her, Fortunée, on those black-and-white harlequin sheets I sewed on *my* sewing machine!!! Do you know what it feels like? Do you know what he's saying by this—'Pssssst! You don't count! YOU'RE INVISIBLE, WOMAN.' *Do you know what that feels like?* Oh Christ Heaven God above, if we could only go back and start out at the beginning! I want that! The beginning of everything!"

"What would you do different at the beginning again?"

"I wouldn't let him turn off, *psssst!* like that, the minute I lost the baby!"

"Whose baby? What baby?"

Biscuit released Fortune's hand, pitching it back at her. "Yes, okay, you know it. Big dramatic thing, hah hah, I hope

173

you're happy . . . you'd have dug it out of me sooner or later . . . it's no big thing, no big cross, yes, okay. Skip Fritchey knocked me up in high school, and we got married graduation week. There! Happy? But I went straight! After my divorce . . . nobody got any tail, no sirree!" She spun away, then turned back to Fortune. "Oh . . . so now you're going to ask me, 'Well, then where have you been at night when you didn't come in? YES, ALL RIGHT, I'LL ADMIT IT THEN! YES, I DID SLEEP WITH MILO!!!"

"I never said you did not."

"YOU WERE ABOUT TO ACCUSE ME OF IT YOUR-SELF! YOU WERE ABOUT TO SAY, 'HAH HAH, COULDN'T EVEN WAIT UNTIL YOUR WEDDING NIGHT'! YOU WERE ABOUT TO SAY I SHOULDN'T BE MARRIED IN WHITE!!!"

"My mouth, Beverly, can make up its own words. And they have not got to be the words a neighbor puts in it."

Biscuit pounced on the couch. She patted it, for Fortune to sit beside her. Gentle, macabre, she began to stroke the ostrich feathers on Fortune's sleeve. "Roomie, darling . . . you've twisted the knife now and had your fun . . . now in return for it . . . just do this: Get Skip and Milo up here together for me . . . and we'll have the wedding albums . . . oh, Milo'll parachute, absolutely. He was always insane, thinking I'd marry Skip again! People *do* do that, you know! Lots of divorced . . . Ah *hah!* That's what you're scared of, isn't it? That I'll marry Skip again!"

"No, I'm not scared."

"After all, Skipper made a little baby embryo inside me. But I flushed that little frog-baby down the toilet in the honeymoon suite at the Honolulu Hilton! Hah hah hah! Did he make a little embryo inside you? Did he do that inside Jeanine? Hah! Don't think he ever got me out of his system! Hah! He loves children and hah hah hah, he still hasn't got a single one!" Biscuit reached up and smoothed Fortune's hair. "Ah, don't get up-tight, Roomie. You and Jeanine can have him. After I'm through with him. In my plan."

Biscuit pushed me back on the couch, Your Honor. Her eyes were knocking around in her head the way a pair of dice will do. I was noticing the mascara cried down black onto her cheeks. And she looked old; she did not look like the bride.

"Listen, Roomie," she whispered. "You help me, then I'll help you . . . when Milo and I are patched up, then I can kind of steer Skip your way, see? I'll help you! You and me! Teamwork! See?"

Fortune said no, she did not see. She did not think the plan would work. Because a person could never say what another human, a man, was thinking up his sleeve to surprise in the opposite direction. ". . . not a good plan. We will think of another one. I will help you. Teamwork!"

"You won't do it?" Biscuit said. She grabbed Fortune's hair and jerked her face up close. She bared her teeth, and her rank breath spread over Fortune's face. "Eh, Pollyanna? I could kill you," she whispered. "I could just kill you."

"You do it and I would kill you back."

✱

The sound of Bob Dylan came from next door's stereo. He had been singing about laying ladies across big brass beds. . . .

. . . And as suddenly as Biscuit had snatched Fortune up,

175

she had released her and spun away. "You frost me," she had said. "You hung-up backwoods professional virgin types frost me so much I could scream."

"Yes, I know," Fortune had said. Her voice was thin. She had removed a handkerchief from her purse then and balled it in her palms to blot them. But the moistness had returned.

Biscuit left and did not come back for several days.

Then the morning Fortune was leaving for Inglewood deliveries, the telephone rang.

Biscuit was calling from the hospital. Cedars of Lebanon in Hollywood. She had had her breasts lifted.

"Knockers up!" she cried into the receiver. "Christ-o, Roomie, what they can't do these days! Come visit me . . . me's wonesome."

Fortune went to the Cedars of Lebanon Hospital. Biscuit peeled back the gauze and showed her (two bare pale centipede scars) each breast. "Wait'll he gets a load of these two high riders! Keep your eyes open, honey, for A-C-T-I-O-N, ACTION!"

20

She said to Biscuit, "You are correct. I am 'hung-up.' About my 'mental monsters.' If I was not 'hung-up' about this thing, plugging, then I would not think and dream about it so much. Dr. Freud says that is the earmark of when a problem bothers a person. (Why do you put on your shocked face? I know these things.) Another earmark: You cannot stop your mind from flipping back to it again and again. And you cannot fib to your mind.

"I know these are situations I have not discussed to you even after one year here. Why? Because you are not like I am. Not in one year. Not in one *light*-year would we be. People have got to be similar to a person is or that person is 'rapping into the wind.' Because they will never understand. You are not like me, and I can tell you that there is not a cell in me that is like you. And do you think I am either like your boyfriend? No, I am not. That is why we all three fight.

"What do you think of this plan? Even with the hat and cigar and birthmark-shaped forehead, this Phil . . . he will do. He wants me to be Mrs. Petzinger, no, do not count your chickens. Stay in your seat. I have laid a long time and concentrated about this. I once upon a time wanted to be a married woman. And my mind used to lurk all day around the idea of love, somebody to love me that did not care about the other 'side of the coin,' plugging. That issue is another situation that is a nuisance to my sleep, but we will leave that issue for a rainy day to talk about.

"And my opinion of the how many thousand men in this club? I cannot lie to you and tell you I know them all— anyway, you know the lies in my eyes by this time, anyway —I do not even know all of them living here at the Villa . . . but I will say about the Dionysus West men I know and see . . . do not get me wrong . . . they are nice. But there is more in this world than 'nice.' The men here, I think, are not for me. Even though I have paid for them, if you look at it that way. They are not for me. Your boyfriend is not either. To my mind, the way he acts and the trying to be cock of the walk, that is not 'my cup.' And as for your ex-husband, the dentist downstairs, Skip Fritchey, he is not for me. He is like a ghost. And nobody could know what is in his heart and head. I could not live my life out wondering and shying back like a whipped dog and talking to somebody that says I talk too much. What do you think of that? But what I am moving around the bush to say is this: This Phil person is, no, not my opinion of the 'cream de la cream mentality.' But he does happen to be an individual that when I wear eyelashes does say I look like a million dollars and that does not try to tell me I talk too much. He is somebody that when persons in this club do not want the sea water dabbed off their face with my handkerchief, Phil knows the earmark of an animal that does not show the good breeding to say, 'Thank you anyway, but no thank you.' Also, Beverly, thank you very much for your idea that Milo should plug me to improve my mental capabilities. That is an idea of yours I say 'Thank you, but no thank you' to.

"But then my mind says, 'Miss Dundy, maybe there is a "kernel" of something in what your roommate says about the subject of "hung-up." '

"I would not plug with a man if he did not love me and know how I am about things first.

"Once upon a time. But I am different now. Except, not enough different. I want to be more still. Because I think my mind will move 'Hell and high water' to make me stop being the way I have been. (Now—and I am not saying this next thing is 'my suit of clothes,' either—I do not want to turn into what befell my friend Ora Russell. Maybe if when she was thirty years old a man made love to Ora, she today would not be 'society's outcast.' Even though today more and more society is saying okay to Ora's kind.)

"I do not like to kick you out of your own bedroom. No, I am not doing this.

"I think a good time for Phil to do this to me would be after the Roman Orgy. That would be like the 'perfect setting.' A 'metaphor,' like they say. What do you think?"

179

21

Eleven o'clock P.M. The pool and courtyard and handball and tennis courts and rec hall are clogged with wandering, traipsing people, wearing sheets and window curtains.

Dionysids were shedding "togas." Some swam nude. Giant styrofoam grapes had fallen into the pool, floated there now. And food lay everywhere on the lawn and tile.

The damp summer air made her "toga" (her peignoir) stick to her skin. She and Phil stepped on melon cubes, olives disemboweled of their pimento, waterlogged sandwiches, and on somebody's hand. Somebody else was making a film. It was Campbell. He leaped around, skidding on plum pits and swearing, juggling his Canon 450, calling it by name. Hordes of people—how many were here?—were drifting across the courtyard, lolling, dancing, passing marijuana, eating, arriving.

She and Phil wandered. He followed her hem, pretending he was drunk, mocking orgiastic decadence. (The brown-and-white toes of his shoes peeped from under his toga; hello! hello! they said with each step. On his head, covering his tuber, he wore a wreath of oleander leaves Fortune had made him.)

Everywhere she went, Fortune spoke with people. With

Tucker Hadiman and his crowd, with Harry, Gary, and Donna and Howard . . . she even talked to "Turk" Mosal-lem. He had flown down, he said . . . "from S.F." . . . for the weekend, in white shoes, in an all-white suit, whiter than the sands of Sicily, a beautiful suit—"Pete Kardin." He stood immobile, like a huge, slick swan, smoking his cigar George Burns style. The diamond ring on his pinky finger . . . when he lighted her cigarette . . . a Ronson engraved *from Kitty con amore*. . . . He looked around and took notes in a pocket notebook and shot off into the dark in his white El Dorado.

Under Campbell's floodlights three girls lay draped in chiffon and wax grapes. Bowls of pudding and boxes of Pudding Tain lay with the girls. The "Imperial flavors." Campbell squalled at the girls to admire the pudding, ogle it for the camera.

*

He grunted when he sat on the bed to remove her high heels. "Now, now, can't keep those on. Those could be dangerous, Cinderella!" He covered her feet up again. "You old scaredy cat!" he said. "Would you believe there's a first time around for all of us, sugar-bud!"

He put his arm around her in the dark and gave her a quick, spirited hug. This made her cartilage respond . . . a small gristly sound. As if . . . her tendons were sighing, shifting . . . preparing.

She hugged him back . . . and kissed the edge of his shoulder. His skin was sandpapery and warm, and she could not keep her mind on what it was she had come here to do in this dark room.

She started to cry. But he did not hear it. Outside, the band was playing, ". . . *bridge over troubled . . .*"

Biscuit stood in front of the bathroom mirror She was painting her new breasts with body paint in Day-Glo letters: *Hi, Daddy, Remember Us?* "Well? How's it going? Sounds pretty quiet in there."

"No. It is not quiet. He is talking. Did you not say he should talk to me first . . . to 'woo' me?"

"Relax. Just relax. Did you shoot up?" Biscuit was trying to correct the *s*.

"Beg pardon?"

"The foam!"

"No. It is still in there. Behind you. Medicine cabinet."

She stepped into the tub and pulled the shower curtain with her, reading the directions on "DAISY *Vaginal Foam.*" . . . the words ran. "*. . . shake the vial well. 2. Place applicator over the top. 3. Hold filled applicator between the cylinder and insert well into the . . .*"

"What's taking so long?" Biscuit said. "Just stick it in there and squirt."

She did. The strange, cool product filled her, and she was frightened. "But," she said, her voice hoarse, "I . . . do not love him."

"Are you crying? Oh, Christ! Crying's for afterward!" Biscuit ripped back the curtain and snatched the can from her. "Now get in there! And don't give me this routine about you don't love him, Fortunée! It's too late for loving! It's not important for you to love him! He loves you! Now *that's* important! Christ-o, how many chances in this lifetime does a woman get a chance to be balled by someone who loves her? But listen . . ." She put down her paintbrush and turned; she smoothed Fortune's hair. "Listen. You can't have somebody on the sidelines coaching forever. But here's one last rule. You make sure he *tells* you he loves you. Yes! Throughout the whole thing! Don't ask him. Don't beg him. You *tell* him he better make you pretty goddamn confident of his love. Language! Words! In your ear!"

"Will it hurt?"

"If he puts it in your ear, yes."

"STOP IT! Tell me!"

Biscuit turned back to the mirror and began to powder her body all over with a light golden powder. "It'll hurt if he doesn't tell you he loves you. If he tells you he loves you, you won't feel a thing."

Phil was smoking in the dark. His cigar coal glowed red as an eye.

He asked her what took her so long. And when he moved over to make room for her, the sheets rustled . . . like rushes, like head-high kunai grass parting, she was running through a field, in her imagination.

"You were gone so long, honey," he said.

"Yes," she said, "I was, honey."

"Was that Biscuit in there?"

"Yes, honey. She is going to surprise Milo. She is painting herself up, her body and things. He is making a film for his agency. She is going to surprise him. Jump in front of it."

"Is she gone?"

"Yes, honey. She is gone now."

22

Very male, Skip Fritchey's silence.

(Did her voice startle him?)

He pulls off his sunglasses for a moment. He rubs his eyes.

It is seven o'clock in the evening . . . summer highways, the sad, heavy light of California summers. She wants to weep . . . it is so sensual. She watches his hands on the wheel . . . his face in profile. He speaks. The sound of his voice is familiar now.

They are on the coast highway. And have passed, by this time, Ventura . . . Carpinteria . . . missions, the Mission of la Purísima Concepción . . . Santa Barbara . . . palm-lined streets . . . tile-roofed homes . . . El Capitan Beach . . . a Volkswagen bus full of hippies blowing in the wind and their babies, parked to look out at the sea . . . more little towns tripping over each other . . . Naples, Tajiguas, Gaviota, Las Cruces, Buellton . . . where youth in their big, virile cars, bright as fingernail polish, cruise Shakey's Pizza Parlors and Orange Juliuses to find out what the long Memorial Day weekend has got to say . . . tonight.

Skip Fritchey's profile is framed by the car window. His face stands in outline against the ocean and the coming evening. The horizon stands still. An illusion, macroscopic, jumps at her: she is a giant taking the sea . . . legs, boots, the sea is a puddle.

The epic beauty of the sea looked like cheap calendar art . . . a picture that could never be brought to life. (Like the Dionne quintuplets and their dishonesty on calendars.

There used to be a grocery store in Hot Springs with such a calendar. The five Dionne girls were hopping out of a canoe on some turquoise Canadian lake. They carried a picnic basket. What hair—lacquer black! The skin? Irreverent and alabaster! Walt Disney's Snow White, that was what the calendar artist pawned off on people. The quints' long, long Pettijohn legs in short shorts—what legs! Their ten zealous Pettijohn breasts fighting against the white, white cotton of their starched blouses! Waists! Wasps! Pettijohn girls . . . Snow White five times.

Then years later, she had seen them in the newspaper. They were photographed in an airport. The Dionne quintuplets: five false young matrons in frumpy winter coats. One was a nun. One was to die soon.)

"Yes, I'd like to hear that," he said.

She told him the joke. "A fat man and a skinny man looked at each other. The fat man started laughing. And he said, 'From the looks of you, there has been a famine in the land.' And the skinny man said, 'From the looks of you, you caused it.'"

The dentist replaced his sunglasses, pushing them up his nose with his index finger. "I don't get it."

She repeated it, and he said: "Who was it who caused the famine?"

She explained the joke to him. "It is what they call 'subtle humor.'"

185

"No wonder I didn't get it." He ran his hands through his hair. Was he bald? Or did he have hair . . . lots of it? What was his hair made of? Dandelions?

❀

She answered him: "To that question I have got to answer this: And this is my answer: When a person has got to keep that eye on that silver lining. (You will not be held with a forthright answer, will you?) All right: When you want something but you cannot for the life of you get your bead on it. Those are the times it is harder to be glad a person came out here than other times."

"Such as?"

"Lots of things! Maybe you want to be a singer but you do not sing good enough to 'go professional.' Or they won't let you."

"Who is they, Fortune?"

"Well, who do you think? Lots of people!"

" 'A Persian's heaven,' " he said, " 'is easily made; 'tis but black eyes and lemonade.' "

"That depends."

"Always."

"A lot of people," she said, "say heaven is having somebody tell you . . ."

❀

"*I love you! I love you! I love you!*"

Those were his exact words, Your Honor.

Fine. Will you tell the audience at this time the blow-by-blow "events" of The "That Night" Affair?

No comment, Your Honor.

186

Bring on Exhibit A, please . . . maybe that will make her "sing." Now. Miss Dundy, do you or do you not recognize this object?

I do.

Would you care to tell our home viewers exactly what it is?

It is my . . . French dressing gown.

AUDIENCE: Gasp! (To one another) Her French dre . . . !

Shut up! Shut up, all of you! You make them shut up, Bert, or my word is "mum" from here on out!

The court will shut up, please. Go on, Miss Dundy.

No. The answer is no, to tell you "gossip buffs" out there. No, I did not lose this. (Holds up her fingers in V sign.) To the lady whispering in the front row, no, madam, that does not stand for "Victory."

AUDIENCE: Whew! (To one another) Would you believe . . . ! Did not lose her . . . !

Ah, but, Miss Dundy?

Yes, Bert?

Then what is this lavender French dressing gown doing . . . OFF YOUR BODY???

AUDIENCE: Gasp!

Oh, you think you are so smart. I will tell you, Mr. Brains! I took it off to climb into the bed itself with the Ex-Stunt Man in question.

Then you were stark . . . ?

No, I was not. I had these high-heeled slippers on. These shoes you see before you now.

And . . . ?

My "partner in the act" instructed for me to remove them for health reasons. His health.

And . . . ?

Then his skin was like sandpaper . . . the shoulder part was.

And . . . ? Miss Dundy?

AUDIENCE: Yikes! Here it comes! What did he do?

Then he told me, "I love you."

AUDIENCE: No. We mean The Other Thing. What did he do with his . . . and with your . . . ?

And, Miss Dundy, what was the situation Mr. Petzinger gave you for his stallment?

There are certain situations you do not know—I can see that! About the contrary-mindedness of a man's blah blah blah at the wrong time that it has got a mind of its own and a man's blah blah blah will not blah blah at the time you say *okay, now!* And then I guess just talking about it was starting to make the situation look up down there with him . . . you know what Dale Carnegie says about "the power of suggestion." And I will tell you that I, by that time, blah blah blah and . . .

Beg pardon, Miss Dundy. But, I mean, did he not even touch you blah blahly first? Or begin any of the blah blah in your book?

What book?

The one in the brown wrapper.

It said For Marrieds. And we were not married, so we will leave that subject for a rainy day. That book is none of your situation so you just put your dirty mind to your next question.

All right. What happened then?

What do you mean, "What happened?" What always happens happened! I left. Crying. I always leave places crying. To prove it does not only happen in books and movies. And I went back to the Roman Orgy . . . and you might think I am lying on this point . . . said I danced "like a dream."

AUDIENCE: But . . . but what about Mr. Petzinger???

I left him crying in my apartment. "Contrary to popular opinion," men *do* cry. Me? I have got about as much use for a man's tears as the judge there has got for that fake white-powdered "judge's" wig he is wearing.

AUDIENCE: (To one another) She is so cruel!

You are turning to stone, Miss Dundy, pure cruel stone. You know that, do you not?

Uh, look, bud . . . when I want comments from you, I will ask for them.

✳

"I'll give you something to daydream about," the dentist said, if that was what all that staring out the window was about. Then he did a startling thing. He snapped on the overhead light and pulled up his shirt. On his side was a scar, rather impressive. He said it was where Biscuit had "poked" him once when she was "upset." (He had said earlier: "You're all right with her, aren't you? She used to be . . . melodramatic sometimes. Maybe she's changed. She's never . . . hurt you, has she? I thought about you with her. You're all right with her?") He dropped his shirt and snapped off the light. "Show's over," he said.

"But I do not want the show to be over! Let me see. Turn on the light. That was not 'whistling Dixie.' What did she use? Why did she do that? Did you bleed?"

"I bled Kool-Aid."

"What did she do that with?" Beg pardon, but . . . The Bread Knife Affair of last . . . December? A person would call *that* "Dixie," I suppose?

"A barbecue fork. Show's over. Your turn. Sing something for me. I heard you singing in the laundry room."

"But I do not want the show to be over."

"You can't always have your way."

(Biscuit's Salome dance with the new breasts "won their point." Fortune had left Phil back in B-12, crying. Campbell was still filming, shouting at the beautiful girls to admire the pudding. Suddenly from the pillars and shadows, Biscuit sprang out into the lights. She had leaped in front of Milo's startled camera. And then later they were back together again and very happy and, she told Fortune, there would probably be a wedding after all.)

When Skip Fritchey had pulled up his shirt . . . his flesh looked soft . . . invertebrate.

A little herringbone of hair . . . it tendrilled up from . . . his navel. Flesh, then.

He was a creature who would one day die. His flesh would go . . . with the meat on the bones of the rest of the world.

Yet . . . he had survived The Barbecue Fork Affair— "wot?"

For a single morbid moment, she had almost asked to touch the scar.

Yes, but what if the scar split open again? What if it sucked your hand in? Throbbing meat! A sucking rosette, right there in his side. (It devours her helpless, curious fingers.)

"NO! I do not sing so terrific."

"Sing," he said.

"You can do this: I can be quiet for the time it takes for one song. And you, in your head, you pretend you are hearing the song. Then when you are done, you tell me how I sounded."

He agreed. Could he request something? Yes, she told him, he could request "Blue Moon." He said that was what he had in mind.

"On your mark," he said. "Get set . . . go."

Blue Moon, she thought, *you saw me standing alone. You knew just what I was there for. . . .*

At the end, she thought out one long and throaty *Blooooooooooo Moooooooooon!* This last soulful note was dying away in her brain. And the dentist said: "Very professional."

Then it was his turn. But he sang out loud:

"I had a sister Sally, she was younger than I am.
Had so many sweethearts she had to deny them.
But as for sister Sarah, you know she hasn't many,
And if you knew her heart she'd be grateful for any.

"Come a landsman, a pinsman, a tinker or a tailor,
Doctor or lawyer, soldier or a sailor,
Rich man or poor man, a fool, or a witty,
Don't let her die an old maid, but take her out of pity."

(She grew taut, waiting for him to stop and start . . . to buckle and apologize, to clear his throat . . . any anemia at all in him.)

"I had a sister Sally, she was ugly and misshapen.
By the time she was sixteen years old she was taken.
By the time she was eighteen, a son and a daughter.
Sarah's almost twenty-nine, never had an offer.

"Come a landsman, a pinsman, a tinker or a tailor,
Doctor or lawyer, soldier or a sailor,
Rich man or poor man, a fool, or a witty,
Don't let her die an old maid, but take her out of pity.

"I never would be scoldin', she never would be jealous.
Her husband would have money to go to the ale-house.
He was there spendin', she'd be home a-savin',
And I leave it up to you if she is not worth havin'."

She sat for a moment. She lighted a cigarette. "You were good," she said. "I cannot lie and pretend 'professional' when in my heart I am saying only, 'He was good.' You are not a 'natural.' What ever happened to her? That Sarah. Did you sing all of it?"

"The tinker took her," he said.

"I myself have never heard of a tinker. I know of a tinker's damn, of course. She should have chosen the doctor."

He said a tinker was a man who mended pots and kettles, and why should Sarah have preferred the doctor? And there followed a discussion about people with that certain subterranean and a Dr. Port Porter, whom Fortune had encouraged. "He went on and was a doctor. I told him I saw it in his hands." And then it worked around to where she said to the dentist, would he just as soon be mending a kettle as a tooth in the head of a human?

He said he might as well be.

"Don't talk that way," she said then.

Ah, he had drifted! How he had drifted away now. Gone! "You don't really expect me to tell you I find any spiritual salvation in dentistry, do you? It's dull as hell. Did you know that among professional people, dentists have the highest suicide rate? Did you know that Esalen offers group therapy for dentists . . . specially designed for dentists? Dentistry, I'm afraid, missed out when the wagons were hitched to the stars. Now, hold on . . . I'm getting to it: Why did I go ahead and be one?"

"Yes!!!"

"Money. I like it . . . and I didn't have the grit for medical school, so I am not a doctor. Money . . . it's nice . . . you can pay alimony and almost never skip a beat . . . and buy pastel cigarettes for people instead of the more pedestrian white-skinned brands. . . . Oh. Eh? So now you're going to lie awake all night mourning the brilliant would-be surgeon who wasted his subterranean voices, taking molds for dentures and scraping tartar. . . ."

"NIGHT!!!! I did not say one single solitary word about lying anywhere tonight! And how come you sang in that song those things and then in the chorus part put in the word 'old maid' instead of the official word instead????"

"What word?"

(Earlier, before nightfall, it was so foggy driving through Big Sur you could not see the edge of the cliff until you came to it. You could hear the surf below. And once in a while there would be a clearing in the fog. And you would see a rock, two seals huddled on it. It began to rain. The plants all around were very bright in the rain, green . . . the chartreuse of the wet century plants . . . and the orange-red of the bark, Monterey Pine, he had said.)

"Oh, never mind," she said. "The subject is boring if you do not know what I mean in the first place."

❀

You invite someone somewhere, you take care of her. You spend the money (*you* earn) on gasoline. You buy her a burger when she complains of hunger. You pay for that burger with your money.

You ask someone to go to San Francisco with you (when you run across her in the laundry room), you see that that person gets fed!

You go up to the drive-in window and put *your* money down on the counter for the food that goes in *her* stomach. You remove the dollar bills from your wallet where your driver's license says SAMUEL D. FRITCHEY. You have got a name! It flashes for a moment, with the bills . . . there is a tiny and thuggish blur of color, your photograph . . . you are A-OK in the eyes of the California Highway Department. You put down that money to pay for that meal because your woman is worth it, by God! And you—your hands are at nine o'clock and six o'clock on the steering wheel—watch her as she munches. She pretends not to notice you noticing her. She wraps her hands daintily around the hamburger. Around the Dixie cup her fingers curl one by one. After her lone dinner, she smokes one of the Vogues you bought her back in Oxnard. (You have lighted her cigarette for her.) She gives you a single, testing glance. What could that look mean, people? It could mean anything! It could mean "The Eyes Have It." Hmmmm . . . you are wondering if she is happy. By God, you think she is! By God, and you will put down one dollar and two dimes any day of the year if you people at this drive-in window, you Jack-in-the-box people, could make her that happy again! Thank you, yourself, and yes, we will come again.

❖

Sausalito:

The sailing togs, Bert, would be fine.

Skip Fritchey's friends: The wife is Kelly, a relief. She is an Easter chicken of a person . . . a silky cap of hair and tiny arms and legs that move around in the soft light of the living room. The husband is Jake; he is big and not such a relief. The saleswoman in the May Co. in L.A. had gone sailing herself once in Balboa and so helped pick out the striped T-shirt and the cap. The room where Fortune slept was full of chintz and braided rugs and copper kettles with dry corn and an old-fashioned sewing machine with straw flowers sprouting out of its drawers and the bed—was it a window seat? a berth?—was set into an alcove of windows. The blankets were deep and soft. Kelly showed her a room full of canvases and wax fruit and a red painting that she called "a sort of Jackson Pollackesque still-life deal." Jake and Skip Fritchey sat talking about friends, business, friends. Kelly went and stood by her giant husband. She smoothed his hair absently with her quick, chick's hand . . . the other pointed out Angel Island out the window . . . the lights. Jake's voice filled the room from the depths of his rib cage . . . came hurtling at her like a bowling ball, and Skip Fritchey was chuckling about somebody they knew a long time ago. The next morning they all went through grottoes and arbors and gazebos, past cottages with stone steps and unlatched gates and shingles, "Clanahan's Cove" or "Nepenthe II." Down to the marina . . . people there threw sponges and ropes, and a lanky girl with hair like highways and legs from magazines jumped into a boat and attacked the mast. Fortune put on her dark glasses.

I put on my "shades."

Skip Fritchey was jumping about too on another sailboat. Its long, white surfaces throbbed in the sun, its porcelain flanks said *Lizajane*. Fortune settled in the well on a cushion. Kelly shooed her off to get ropes. The little chick was fussing and harrying cabinets and things with a sporty female confidence. They probably do not even permit smoking around here. "Person allowed to smoke around here?" Skip Fritchey swooped down from somewhere in bare feet and hairy legs. He moved her aside wordlessly and untied the . . . "tiller." Then he was gone again to the farthest reaches of the boat, with Jake. Yes, fine, all right, fine. As long as the ants want to be so standoffish . . . we grasshoppers aboard will sit and mind to our own, enjoy the sun. She closed her eyes, almost, and studied him. He had peeled off his shirt. In the morning light The Barbecue Affair scar looked rather untheatrical. The striped boxer swim trunks fit him politely enough. He had not been so rude as to wear that other kind, "Jockey." With their "second-skin" rudeness. But she was on guard. A treacherous puff of wind . . . come along . . . rudely . . . lift the leg of Skip Fritchey's . . . swim trunks, and then show the lax . . . *turkey waddles!* She looked hard at his body . . . the hair on his thighs—oh, the bitter order of maturity! She looked away. But remembered the lines of his lean back—he was lankyish himself, after all— working the sails. They drifted far out onto the bay. The day was brilliant. It blinded, it drugged. "Hello, Sealegs," Skip Fritchey said to her at some point. She watched houses and trees go by far away and other sailboats, like butterflies that dipped and glided. "Hello, Captain Blood," he said at another point. (What if he could guess all the most private and sensational things about her? Her fantasies . . . her

mastur-what, Miss Dundy? . . . her foolishness and her
. . . Bert, what if he could guess all the times in my life I
have been a fool?) But she had paid good money for the hat.
Yes, but, "Anchors Aweigh," indeed! What anchors away
have you ever dropped? DY-GUY . . . what you do is you
go in a shop and pay your money. He was watching her,
working the tiller. He looked away. She shook her head. The
little cotton sailor cap—"Anchors Aweigh" on the brim—blew
away and was swallowed by the boat's churning wake. They
docked at Tiburon. "Sam's" the place was . . . outdoors.
People ate and talked at tables in the sun. She wanted postcards. Skip Fritchey took her by the back of the neck to buy
the postcards she wanted. On a giant unwieldy postcard she
wrote: "Hello, Apache Junction, Arizona and Buck Springs
Hotel and Mrs. Shortt here I am in the city by the Bay San
Francisco make an effort yourself to journey here to solve
your aches and tribulations better than that mineral bath."
She wrote some more things and signed it F. Dundy and her
friend Dr. S. Fritchey. Meanwhile, Skip Fritchey, too, was
writing on one of the giant postcards . . . was it to Jeanine?
He was writing and writing . . . it was taking him forever.
What was he writing that took such a long, fastidious twenty
minutes? Fortune moved away, as if in search of stamps . . .
but she remembered him writing. As he was writing, he had
looked so sterile . . . had vanished into himself. And she
was so jealous of the postcard. . . . They bought stamps
and walked down narrow streets to look for a mailbox . . .
Saturday passing, crowds of barefoot teen-agers and bicker-
ing tourists . . . Skip Fritchey pulled her out of the way of
a Vespa . . . beautiful girls that all looked like Jane Fonda
floated by, they wore pastel sunglasses and rings on their

197

thumbs . . . they leaned on their shoulder-strap purses, pausing to peer in boutique windows, cocked on their long flamingo legs . . . passing, too, runty men, Nikon cameras bouncing against their bellies . . . pubescent girls in threes, swaying in leather and suede fringe, transistor radios clamped on their ears . . . their nodule breasts peaking under their T-shirts as they scuffed and dodged . . . giggling and exaggerating, eating candy apples and, when they laughed, spitting the ruby fragments onto the sidewalk. An older boy in a thistly beard and bad-ass jacket followed them, straining to be noticed . . . walked in a springy, high-school drop-out walk. She awakened at two A.M. The house was quiet, dark. She lay there, planning to tell him there was somebody scratching at her window. And if he said what a lie, she would cry, yes, that is perfect with you! He can claw me to death, but, blah blah not believe that, no, you would say I am moaning to get attention. She got out of bed. The floor creaked; twenty minutes later she was only as far as the kitchen, taut, pausing with each step. He was sleeping. On the couch just inside the living-room door. It was too dark to see. She swallowed. Her own saliva crackled in her eardrums. "Heyyyyyyyyyyyyyyy?" she said and ran away, grazing her elbow. Five minutes passed. No response. She got out of bed and did it again. And finally a third time, stepping a few feet into the living room. She said, "Uhnnnn-nnnnnnnnnnnnnnnnnnn." His blankets rustled. She drew herself against the refrigerator. Then ran through the dark. "Fortune?" He was in her room now. "What the hell's going on?" He sat on her bed and rather automatically began stroking her hair. She pretended sleep. He yawned. "Jesus, what time is it?" he said to himself. "I know you're not asleep." Her eyelids began to twitch. She whimpered and settled . . . pretending dreaming, inquietude . . . she hid her eyes in the pillow. "Well," he said, "if she doesn't wake up in the next ten seconds, I guess I'll go on and leave her here alone with the Boogie Man. I guess she doesn't need me." Now was the moment she was supposed to sit up and accuse him but she remained still. Yet pretending to be asleep, she whipped her face around, her heart thundering. He lay his hand lightly on her eyelids, as if she were a corpse. His hand felt dead . . . he sucked in his breath, privately. The sound had an unnerving quality to it. It was weary, universal. It was filled with an exquisite sadness . . . and it grieved her beyond sensation. In one swift thrust, she sat up and clamped herself around his neck. She clutched him with a cosmic, melodramatic ferociousness . . . until he ceased to be a living thing but became a symbol of living things. She embraced him so consummately, the impression was one of clutching at herself. "Oh," he whispered, stroking her back. (She had clutched him until her arms quivered . . . and she had begun to cry. This seemed to come as no surprise to him.)

23

His breathing moved the sheets as he slept. Although he lay on top of the eiderdown comforter. The dim light of dawn fell on his bare back and his puffed-out shorts. He was sunburned. And his skin gave off that captured heat.

He had gathered her to him. . . . Now he slept, a mortal sleep. His boxer shorts poofed out, wrinkled. He had kissed her . . . was it many times? Or once . . . ? They had either been kisses . . . or they were tales and spells and conjurations moving over her face as running water might have . . . his pity, his attention, all over her face. In the five minutes before he had fallen asleep, he touched her breasts . . . hesitantly. In response she had quivered like a tuning fork. In the middle of a sentence—one of hers—he had fallen asleep. At first she lay there, raw with disbelief . . . and quite insane with love and loving. She wanted to awaken him. She grew jealous of his sleep. Should she have invited him under the covers? Should he have invited *himself* to get under them? With his kisses, he had loomed over her like a shaman.

Gingerly then she located her head next to his on the pillow. There was the smell of his sleep! Warm . . . and it reminded her of an Army surplus store. If she touched him

—pip! like that—he would awaken. The idea of her power occurred to her. She could bring about change in him. Even so simple a change as drawing him back to consciousness from his selfish, abysmal sleep. She left the bed and, in ecstasy, went outside into the garden. She climbed through an intricacy of bushes and vines, crushing poppies and not meaning to. . . . She peered in at the window bed.

His head lay on the pillow, only a few inches from the windowpane. In the dawn light she studied his hairline . . . nose, his mouth, his jaw slack and distressing in sleep, his chin, his throat textured with whisker stubble. The leaves' shadows, the gray-green light, the dawn patterns mottled his back. Dappled, he slept blending with the light, the paisley quilt. His arm was bent strangely under his chest, a strange, uncharacteristic wrenching of his body line. Her eyes darted across his back . . . the puffed-out, almost childish undershorts . . . then his legs. One was straight, the other bent. Almost as if he were leaping. In a frozen, horizontal leap, he sleeps suspended! He seemed so . . . *excellent*. She put her hand on the window. She could hear nothing: possibly love had struck her deaf. (She remembered, however, his "Oh." He had sounded like a girl when he stroked her. Stroking her and kissing her, he had been so *uncritical!*) She crouched down. Through the glass, her gaze moved back to his face. It was so near . . . only the glass . . . his lips are parted, viscid in sleep. Cracked, peeling, from sailing, wind, sun. They reveal his imperfect teeth. Those lips . . . flaking, scratching like insects' legs, scaly . . . they had skimmed over the inside of her arm. On the outside of her arm they riffled the down there like young grass . . . lightly, harmlessly, they sojourned on her skin. They had moved on to kiss her cheek ("Yes. Yes," he said), her hair. Those shredding, uncritical kisses . . . and he had begun to rock her.

. . . he was so imperfect! The cracked lips! The pores! The ragged eyebrows! These flaws! This same defiance of perfection . . . was excellence! He seemed one jump ahead of his body . . . his looks . . . and other people's opinions of that body, those looks. He was sublime. His eyebrows . . . his pores . . . his whiskers . . . and his forehead: behind this plate of bone lay his brain in gentle coils. Even to imagine his brain like intestines made him stunning, magnificent. Now she noticed a single vein. It bulged down the center of his forehead, a purplish, pleasant, intelligent-looking vein. A pipeline, draining his dreams off his dreams . . . as he slept. She nearly fainted with love.

Blink. He opened his eyes then. Blink. She did not move. Blink blink. Nor did he. His lips closed. He blinked his eyes once more, staring into her eyes. He closed his eyes, as if in pain. He opened them. Through the window, he looked back into her gaze.

The light was changing. Now she could see her own reflection in the window . . . her reflected eyes superimposed upon his eyes, opaque. She tilted her head, as if to erase him. In his eyes the melancholy pulled at her like quicksand; his gaze was sucking her into a vortex of something he mourned . . . his eyes drew her into his brain . . . absorbing . . . like a blotter . . . the strain of her own awakened sadness . . . a tremor. He smiled. And then that left his face. And they continued to gaze into each other's eyes through the glass. When she went back into the "Early American" room, he was gone and she lay down and could smell where his head had been on the pillow.

24

Report:

The "boxer" kind, Bert, he sleeps in his underwear. The frills of life do not interest him. Men brush over these things, you know. They drink milk straight from the carton in the refrigerator is one example that they do not do the things other people take a lifetime attending to. Use a *glass?* Wear *pajamas?* It is all part of the "crap" they cut out of their lives. I could have told you he sleeps in his underclothing. He is a man.

25

It was raining. They were at a motel, somewhere along Highway 101. They had driven through beach upon beach, gauzy miles bound by mist, dotted with seals. Now Skip Fritchey was telling her to sign the register. He got the bags out of the car. She was signing her name, and the clerk said, he thought there was mail for her. He lay a giant postcard down. It was *the* postcard.

To Whom It May Concern:

I have come to hear the beat of myself
with my cheek pressed against the door
of our reign, old man.

To:
Miss Fortune Dundy
Meson Maravilla
Morro Bay, Calif.

And I have been reminded off again and
redistributed among my visions. These
broad pale flowers, issue of my eyelids,
suggest old others, those waxy and
euphoric on a pearlized altar that put
me once on the budding side of breathing,
    the ones smothered small and gold
in a marketplace
    against my legs then as long as
cold-stemmed roses.

That cluster became so intense the
aroma from our many seaport handfuls
condensed and fell
like all the droplets of new love,
like tiny flowers on frosted tea cakes
that whetted my restlessness
    grown green with loving.

Today I counted myself.
I counted myself as close to lilacs as
the after-talcum of my bath, it settles
in the creases of my body, this corrugated
castle where once I was queen.
I come to tell you it is I, sire,
who am no more warm nor round nor timeless
than the sun that came forth
    upon the kingdom.

  The clerk opened an album with a colored photograph of
each room. There were thirty . . . The Louis XIV Room, The
Alpine Room, The Castilian Room . . .
  She chose The Safari Suite.

  Outside the drops fell on the porch, splatting, falling like
molten lead.
  The place was full of heads . . . caribou, jackals, a leopard. An elephant's leg . . . with toenails . . . was a trash
can. A zebra in porcelain, pony-sized, stood in one corner.
The canopies over each bed—animal skins . . . the walls
bore real crossed spears, hide shields, an oil painting, more
heads . . . the television set peeked out of foliage. The
shower in one of the bathrooms was made of flat rocks . . .
the water tumbled out of the overhead stone ledge, a jungle

cascade . . . even the telephone was painted in zebra stripes. . . . (Campbell answers at B-12 . . . Biscuit is washing her hair but he will tell her to call Circe . . . yes, to tell Circe: not tomorrow, but day after tomorrow, yes. He calls her "Champ" and asks where she is and she tells him Morro Bay and the name of the motel . . . and Campbell says he can hear thunder. Yes, she says, is it raining in Los Angeles too?) In the car, whenever he spoke, his voice had come to her down a long tunnel. He had touched her hand, as he drove, her hair . . . and all this had made her hallucinate . . . sucked into his compassion, his integrity, at the point of touch, a victim of his suction . . . and she would be with him forever.

Mistrustful now, blissful, she looked out the window of The Safari Suite into the rain dropping like nickels.

＊

She had tried to imagine what it would feel like to be dead. By closing her eyes and trying to wipe all thought from her mind. But . . .

. . . Rusty, of all people, appeared. What did Rusty do during the day? Where did her prowling take her? Did she grocery-shop and menstruate like other women? Someday Rusty would be dead and filed under a headstone at Woodlawn. People would read Ora Russell and think she was someone's grandmother. Rusty's grave would lie next to a man and wife, married fifty years. Rusty had had nobody to spend eternity with. So she scrooches up her grave alongside the golden anniversary couple; Rusty was like a mongrel dog that took up with people and followed them home. When it rained, it would rain on all three graves. The rain would forgive Ora Russell for being society's outcast as it blessed the dead man and his wife for being ordinary and true to their phylum. Phil would visit the graves . . . because he was just that way. Maybe he was only out at the cemetery with flowers for his mother. But walking back to his Landrover, his glance skips across the graves. Ora Russell, he says . . . hmmm, she lies alone . . . buried some years ago. Then Phil wonders about maggots and decomposition and pictures the corpse's head rotting on satin. Wonder what she died of? he says to himself. That married couple next to her reached their eighties. Donna and Howard come tramping the white gravel paths. Their children are obese but childish. The family lugs a picnic larder, heads for the park. This graveyard is only a shortcut. The children somersault on the graves. Donna threatens to whip them. Beneath all this, Ora Russell and the two dead neighbors, rotting, feel the earth jarred by fat children. Donna and Howard's Dalmatian raises his leg against a marble headstone. Spot! *Spot!* Bad dog! Heel! Heel! Honestly, Howard, sometimes that dog can be so insensitive. Sally! Dick! Jane! Now you kids straighten up or we have got to give you what-for again. Oh, Howie, look here! Here is where Fortune Dundy *née* "Fortunée" is buried! Is that not cute? Look at that, would you?—*Here Lies F. Dundy of Dionysus West, Friend to Mankind, Swinging Single, Died a Virgin, 1970* A.D. Oh, gosh, what that club will not think of next! SPOT!!! Spot, really! She was a friend of ours.

AND NOW, WILL YOU WELCOME . . . ! Tell them out there for us, Miss Dundy, now that you Have Arrived

. . . what does it feel like to be a "Woman of the World"?

Well, I would just like to "rap" a minute with all those girls wondering out there in Wonderland, those kids wandering around in their "unnatural state" at the *tail* end of their twenties—hah hah hah! Girls: There is no secret to it! You just start out on the right foot and go on from there . . . for, oh, until you cannot wait any longer. In some "advanced cases" you have got your typical person that is waiting for "Mr. Right." But, Girls, here is what I have got to say: Do Not Be Afraid of the "*Misterioso*" Part. The best things in life are "*misterioso*," and I want to tell you.

Well, Fortune Dundy, we surely do thank you for being with us. And I know that all the maidens out there blah blah blah, by golly, for making the crooked way straight!

Good-by . . . and well, thanks yourself, Bert! Oh . . . and Bert?

HE: Yes?

F. DUNDY: Here. I will not be needing these little things. I am not "into" orchids so much any more. Why do you not just pass them along to the First Runner-Up? Thank you just the same.

HE: *What???* You are planning to walk out of here? Just like that? "De-Flowered," like they say?

F. DUNDY: (Clever laugh. Followed by "mystery" laugh.)

HE: LET US HEAR IT, NOW! There she goes, folks!

F. DUNDY: Help, help, the sky is falling!

WONDERFUL DOCTOR, SCARRED BY FORKS AND LIFE: I love you! You always hurt the one you love! Am I hurting you?

F. DUNDY: (.)

208

Mama
Mama
Mama
MamaMamaMamaMamaMama
MamaMamaMamaMamaMama
Mama
Mama
Mama
Mama
Mama
Mama
Mama
Mama
Mama
Mama

*

He embraced her under the covers. Slowly. As if he were swimming around her. Captain Blood, he called her. (Even in his weakness of euphoria . . . there was that inherent dignity of his. An austerity he contradicted every time he kissed her or stroked her.) Nothing had happened yet . . . since she had appeared in his bed. They only lay and stared into each other's eyes. She could neither breathe . . . nor hear . . . nor could she speak. He closed his eyes then and turned his face away. He swallowed, and this sounded in her ear then. He took her hand and placed it upon his neck and then he turned his face back to her. He said her name and tears came into his eyes. The bed, if you turned a switch at the night table, shuddered and vibrated.

She said nothing but lay with her legs entwined in his. The window was open, no screen, and the rain blew in sometimes from outside.

.   .   .

First she had been in the other half of the suite. Alone, in the other double bed.

He had turned the color television set onto the Dick Cavett Show for her and she plugged the earphone into her ear. He had gone into the other room, and she watched his light go out. She tuned out the remote control and sat watching Dick Cavett's guests laugh soundlessly and cross and recross their legs. Drunk with love, she lay in the canopied bed like this for a few moments, stroking the ostrich feathers at her throat and studying the glazed eyes of a snarling leopard. It was so very dead; it looked impotent, absurd. She then had turned up the sound on Dick Cavett and unplugged the earphone.

Then she was in the other part of the suite, in Skip Fritchey's embrace, his bed.

Her suspended breaths were like words . . . or the spaces between them . . . they struck his sunburned arm and were warm, like the arm.

For a while nothing was said. Then his voice rasped her name in the hot, airless gap between their faces. He began . . . that he ". . . ache? Why do I? What is it . . . you . . . makes me feel lost? You're brave. I'd like to be as brave as you are . . . I've always thought that about you. That you were brave in an unbrave milieu. I don't want . . . do anything . . . I . . . maybe lie here. Or maybe scream. Oh Jesus, I'm euphoric. I could die tomorrow, it wouldn't matter. You're so calm . . . so quiet . . . I thought you would be nervous. You always surprise me . . . you always have . . . ah, I want to kiss your cheek. Oh . . . you are . . . and I do love you. Oh. What? . . . Your spine . . . it

slopes . . . it takes a quarter . . . there on the night table
. . . you have to put it in the slot. . . ."

And later, he rose over her and like a shroud came down
upon her, for the first time, and she said the words he had
told her to say: I am a brave soldier. Only it must have been
a scream. He stopped. Her lips were dry.

He suggested they take a shower instead. They would wait
a while. There was no hurry. And on the way to the rocks
he said something, some joke, Tarzan, and then she said
something else . . . "Oh, that," he said, "no, that's no problem. That was gone a long time ago. It dried up and fell out
and blew away like a candy wrapper . . . once when you
were riding a bicycle . . . or a horse . . . or daydreaming.
But there's no hurry. No hurry." Dick Cavett was gone . . .
and now a movie with Ernest Borgnine . . . She said she
was almost a soldier and he said, yes, not long, not far to go
. . . he stopped and scrubbed her feet, lifting each one . . .
the water fell upon his curved, sunburned back. He rose,
slippery. He held her neck as if to strangle her. He gathered
her to him under the water. She kissed him. She felt the
shower on her eyelids, and his limp, incidental penis against
her hip. She kissed his integrity and his dignity and his compassion, his imagination, and his patience . . . and she
kissed herself in him and his self revealing itself in her. She
kissed him and kissed him. "My love," he said. "Oh . . . my
love." *Whump! Whump!* went his back suddenly; his back
and muscles had a voice. He fell away. "Son of a bitch," he
said, spurting blood. He was down now, on the floor, half in
the shower, half out. Biscuit stood over him, wet, shooting
into him. He squirmed and coughed and lay still. Fortune

reached out her hand and her finger, the very tip, was shot off and then Biscuit turned and shot twice more into Skip Fritchey, emptying the pistol. The body twitched.

"Beverly?" Fortune said. "Is that you? Is that you that shot him?"

It was so clear that he was dead. She did not even have the impulse to go to him . . . as she would have thought.

He flinched one last time and gurgled; the fingers of one of his hands curled and uncurled, like a flower. The body made a sound again . . . but it was not a word.

She looked at his staring face. Two tears stood stillborn in his eyes. Everything in the bathroom glinted, austere, whiter than a hospital. A hairpin . . . her own? From somebody who had been in The Safari Suite before? The cleaning woman's? . . . the hairpin lay on the white tile floor, rusting. Rust or blood? She had stabbed Biscuit to death with one of the African spears. Blood like bright enamel paint lay in carmine pools around her body and the dentist's. A speckled arc of it crossed the mirror. She lay down full-length to rest a moment, her cheek flat against the floor, as if she were listening for a heartbeat in the cold, wet tiles.